SILENCE IS MY MOTHER TONGUE

Also by Sulaiman Addonia

The Consequences of Love

SILENCE IS MY MOTHER TONGUE

A Novel

SULAIMAN ADDONIA

Graywolf Press

Published by arrangement with the Indigo Press, London.

This publication is made possible, in part, by the voters of Minnesota through a Minnesota State Arts Board Operating Support grant, thanks to a legislative appropriation from the arts and cultural heritage fund. Significant support has also been provided by Target, the McKnight Foundation, the Lannan Foundation, the Amazon Literary Partnership, and other generous contributions from foundations, corporations, and individuals. To these organizations and individuals we offer our heartfelt thanks.

Published by Graywolf Press
250 Third Avenue North, Suite 600
Minneapolis, Minnesota 55401

www.graywolfpress.org

Published in the United States of America

ISBN 978-1-64445-033-8

2 4 6 8 9 7 5 3 1
First Graywolf Printing, 2020

Library of Congress Control Number: 2019956895

Cover design: Kyle G. Hunter

Cover images: iStock

To the girls – my playmates in our refugee camp: we had no toys but only our imagination to play with. Our playfulness was our painkiller in that place of scarcity. I thought of you, and the childhood friends we saw buried, whenever I came close to giving up.

This book is for you.

We know absolutely nothing about the appearance of the Celestial Stag (maybe because nobody has ever had a good look at one), but we know that these tragic animals live underground in mines and desire nothing more than to reach the light of day.

'The Celestial Stag', from *The Book of Imaginary Beings*
Jorge Luis Borges

THE TRIAL

Cinema Silenzioso

The night Saba's trial was announced by the camp's court clerk, I was sitting on a stool in front of my cinema screen. Cinema Silenzioso.

Dusk fell over the thatched roofs. A full moon appeared over the camp I viewed through my screen. Light like thick blue ink splotched on the walls and between the alleys, wood-burning stoves glowed red.

I saw the clerk riding his donkey in the dusty narrow streets. His silhouette skittered among the huts.

You are requested to attend the trial of Saba, the clerk declared through his megaphone. The courtroom is moving to the cinema compound.

On hearing her name I leapt to my feet. The sketch of Saba I was holding dangled above the open furnace next to me. The charcoal strokes defining her nipples glistening in the light of the smouldering fire. I looked at Saba's compound appearing through the screen like a picture. She was nowhere to be seen. Her lime tree stood frozen against the clay colours of the surrounding huts. Grasshoppers hung off the slant of sugarcane leaves in front of her hut's window.

When I first built my cinema inside my compound, I was inspired by the memory of the forty-five round lights on the facade of the Italian Cinema Impero in Asmara, where I worked before I fled to the camp. I made my cinema screen from one large white sheet I ironed and tied to two wooden poles embedded in the ground, with a big square cut out in the middle. I placed it near the crest of the hill on top of which my compound was located. Many thought I had done so to let the full light of the stars and the moon cascade over the performers on the open screen, the camp behind them existing in isolation. Like a mural, an artifice of a bygone era.

The real reason, though, was different. From the hilltop, looking through the screen when the light was right, you could see into Saba's compound, fenced on three sides, letting the hill on which the cinema stood act as the fourth fence. I could watch her all the time, her world a part of mine.

The trouble was that I, like many, had bought into the illusion that the sheet was an actual screen and that everything inside it was a real film – scene after scene made in a faraway place. Illusion nested in my life with each day passing in front of my cinema. And the two worlds, the real one in which Saba lived, and the virtual one of the film I watched, where all is not what it seems, existed in harmony.

I saw her cooking, reading, ironing, working, teaching adults to read and write, but I also watched her do what people do out of each other's sight. And as I talk to you now, a random selection of images of her replays in my mind. There was that evening she spent masturbating behind the latrine, as her brother cooked doro wot stew for her and her husband.

But that scene is blurred by another one. There she sat on her heels in front of the large curved stone placed on the ground, and, as she crushed the grain on the big stone, her bottom rose off her heels, and the hem of her black dress fluttered as she leaned her shoulders forward to grind the grains by moving smaller stones backward and forward over them. Her burnt thighs were glowing like candles, her history of wounds concealed by the cloud of white flour coiled in front of her and into which her head entered and exited, her hair turned white. Saba's flour-dusted face exists in my mind next to her made-up face on the night of her wedding, when she sat next to her middle-aged husband wearing a dress once owned by a dead woman. Everything is recycled in our camp, happiness as well as despair.

And I keep returning to her wedding night. I still shiver at the thought of her brother tiptoeing his way to the marital bedroom long after the music had died and the guests had departed to leave the bride and groom to consummate their marriage. How he twisted as he placed an ear to the wall.

Now, I was thinking about Saba, her crime, her impending trial, when she exited her hut and appeared on the screen in her black dress, her other skin. Sitting back on my stool, I returned to watching my cinema and Saba through it. She perched on her bed under her lime tree, a book in hand. The oil lamp by her bedside flickered. Saba always slept outside in the open air, and I would watch her every night as the moon and stars cascaded over her taut skin.

I assumed she would read her book now. She'd been rereading Chekhov's *The Lady with the Dog*, which the English coordinator had left in our camp with his British newspaper, as if by reading it over and over again she would have an equally happy ending to her own love story. But whom did she love?

The screen of my cinema quivered. Saba turned on her radio. Music blurted out into the silent evening. And moments later, as I placed a pot of milk on the open furnace, I heard footsteps. When I raised my head, I saw her walking up the hill towards me, gliding like a ghost among the shrubs and cactuses. As I leaned forward, I nudged the open furnace.

Saba, in her black dress and ankle-strap sandals, stood next to the multicoloured chair in front of me, a bag in her hand. She looked like a character escaped from an Italian film. A figment of my imagination? I could see her though. Smell the perfume of her body.

She walked away from the screen and hung her black dress over the low branch of a hibiscus tree near the edge of the hill. She returned to the screen naked and sat on the multicoloured plastic chair, the same chair on which performers sat to tell stories, to recall life in our homeland before the war, before our exile. In the cinema, I often pleaded with performers that they were free to say and do what they wanted. But people remained bound by their exiled condition. I knew I didn't need to remind Saba of this.

Ants climbed her toes, pedicured by Hagos the evening before.

Saba retrieved a pair of scissors from her bag and began cutting away at her hair. The white-silver glow of the bright sky poured onto the screen. As the long strands of her black hair fell on the floor, she stared at me through her dense eyelashes. The whites of her eyes were disturbingly clear.

The wind stirred. Sparks flared up in all directions. The milk in the pot boiled up, turning into a fluffy dome of white spilling over, putting out the flame.

Saba stretched her arm through the gap in the screen and took the cigarette I had lit in the open furnace before her arrival. I wished I could hold her hand for just a moment, but to do so would mean calling into question all that I had believed until then. This is a cinema in a refugee camp, I told myself. Saba is an actor in a film made in a foreign land.

She puffed out cigarette smoke. Her face vanished in the cloud. Saba has a history of disappearance, and reappearance. And for a moment no one existed on the screen. Not even the camp. Saba was a lie, this camp an illusion. But the fumes of neglect rose from the camp behind her, rooting me to reality. The smell of damp yellow thatches, of dung-filled mud walls, of the open field we all shared as a toilet where I had encountered Saba so many times.

An eagle landed on the hibiscus tree inside my cinema, opening its beak as if Saba's black dress was laced with bloodied memories, her flesh the thread holding this fabric together.

The moon disappeared behind the clouds. Saba vanished in this momentary darkness, her face resurfacing as she drew on her cigarette. But darkness always returned in this place. Lamps ran out of oil. Batteries expired. Half our lives were spent in darkness.

Talk, I urged Saba. Please say something.

And she did, after the eagle flew away. I used to believe, she said. I believed that, although people flee their homeland, leave their belongings behind, our traditions stay glued to our core. They escape with us to wherever we go.

She paused and raised her eyes to the sky.

What was she trying to tell me? What was she trying to prepare me for? Did this have anything to do with the trial?

A gust of wind whipped life back into the hissing charcoals. Sparks hit the side of my face. Tears welled up in my eyes. It was I who encouraged members of the audience to hold no fear when they entered my screen. Instead of retelling their tragic stories in the camp, I urged them to recount their dreams so that they turned into fantasy in this remote place. Once they were within the confines of my cinema, they were not refugees bound by their exile; instead, they could say or do whatever they wanted. Because, I told them again and again, you are characters in a film made in a free place somewhere far away.

And some believed it. I remember the boy who told of his fantasy about his uncle's wife. His brothers dragged him out of the screen through the hole in the sheet and beat him unconscious. Or the girl who was to be married off by her parents, but who became captivated by the illusion of my cinema, declaring the name of her true love the moment she stepped inside. Her parents disowned her.

And now my innovation had infected Saba too. I wasn't ready to hear the truth. I picked up a chunk of charcoal and stood up ready to hurl it at the sheet. Burn down my cinema for good and with it my fantasy, and Saba, and all the fragmented scenes of her I had collected and woven together. The scenes through which I had survived. My life was a mirage because Saba was a mirage.

Turn off the lamp, she said.

I dropped the ball of fire. And when I did as she asked, she faded. But her purple thighs and the chair under her dark body shimmered in the moonlight. Half of her turned into a sitting silhouette, as if she was the negative of a picture, the real person behind the image being somewhere else.

Whenever she inhaled on the cigarette, her features emerged inch by inch, redrawn out of darkness, in the way she wanted, as if she were ready to replace with her own words all the stories told about her.

But then came the knocks I had been dreading. Loud and persistent. Jamal, we know you are in there.

I could hear the court clerk shouting through the door.

Jamal, open the door at once. Are you talking to yourself again?

I slipped my hands through the screen, touched Saba's purple thighs, and drew my breath from the violence printed on her skin, as if confronting her wounds was the only way to confirm her existence, and challenge her invisibility in my mind.

Jamal, open the door now before I break it, the clerk said.

Saba zoomed out of the cinema screen. I followed the tip of her cigarette as she strode to the hill. The clouds scattered.

Her trial began under a bright sky.

And as soon as I opened the gate to my cinema, the clerk stepped in, followed by droves of people.

Girls carrying firewood trudged in line. The firewood on their backs squeaked. Behind them, old men in turbans and with gabis swathed around their blazers stopped, blocking the entry. They reminisced about Asmara. Since I arrived here, and every time I close my eyes, said the eldest among them, I see Mussolini in the central boulevard he named after himself.

They held hands and moved forward together, facing the memories in unison. Buonasera, Jamal, they greeted me as they sat in the front row. A herder showed up while still shaking her goatskin in which she churned milk into tesmi. The smell of butter receded when a sex worker – face covered in black seed oil perfumed with cinnamon – appeared in the doorway.

Asmarino boys entered my compound with cardigans tied around their necks, still holding their playing cards. The joker among them mimed an explosion with his hands as women balancing jerrycans full of river water on their heads arrived through the gate. The women, though, smiled, threw their hips to the side, arms akimbo. Their chattering stopped when an eighty-something-year-old woman, whose daughter and granddaughter had been martyred at the front fighting for our country's independence, arrived on her donkey. The animal brayed when the grandmother dismounted from its back.

I stood and gave up my chair to this woman whose womb had once upon a time sheltered lionesses. Saba is free, she said, squeezing my hand. Saba is free. A woman is free before her country is liberated.

I kissed her forehead.

The judge and the elders had yet to arrive. One woman lamented the peculiarity of putting each other through trial, as if life in the camp wasn't doing this already.

The crowd soon laughed again though, when our camp's barber asked me if I had finally lost my virginity to the uncircumcised woman working at the aid centre, whom I helped translate English to Tigrinya and Arabic. I wanted to bring a quick conclusion to what would no doubt be a long discussion by revealing I had lost my virginity instead to an uncircumcised man. I said no such thing, though. Instead, I smiled and kept the mask of pretence going.

My silence intensified the curiosity. Eyes continued to probe the disguise over my face. I firmed my posture to affirm my manhood, countering the femininity that infected my bones like ants digging holes in the ground. Somehow, I collected my fragmented body into one, and stood straight as a doum palm tree.

The judge will arrive soon, said the clerk.

And, as if to kill time while waiting for the trial to begin, a man handed me and the son of our Sufi imam a sword each. Time, the saying goes, is like a sword: if you don't cut it, it cuts you.

The mystic and I were requested to jump closer to the divine, closer to exhilaration, and return to this ground bearing his love. The imam's son and I jumped, elevating ourselves high above the compound, the camp, and glided towards the berry-coloured sky, our blades clashing mid-air, and together we tapped our weapons into the monotonous sky until it bled. Dusk arrived. Blood filled the curves of the thatched roofs.

My friend and I fell back to the ground giggling. We hugged, our swords behind the other's back. In this isolated, neglected place, it's your friend you must watch out for, Saba had once said to me.

Recalling her words, I dug the heel of my hand into my friend's shoulder blade, just as he did mine. We marked each other's presence in the other's memory and, laughing, we returned to our seats.

But where is the judge? I asked, hoping to put an end to this charade once and for all. Not that I had had enough of my fellow refugees. On the contrary. It wouldn't be an exaggeration to say it was their merciful solidarity that kept me alive during the first weeks and months of life in the camp. Some families allowed me to share their children's beds and their few spare items of clothing, so that at night both their children and I slept naked as our clothes dried outside. Our limbs intertwined, sweat glued us together.

And for a long time, before I had inherited my hut from a man who had drowned in the river, I slept in different huts and laid my head on the same pillow as a poet, a rapist, a widow, an adulterer, a fantasist and compulsive liar, an imam, a homosexual, a priest, a closet transvestite, a man who molested his son, a mother who beat her children until her rage was engraved on their skins, and for a while, I dwelt with a young widow who spent her nights parked on the ground of her hut on all fours, surrendering her naked body to the ghost of her deceased husband, so I went to bed with the smell of her yearning sex filling my lungs.

These people's dreams, their fears and crimes, became mine. I lived wondering whether I would end up a dreamer, a wanderer between countries and lovers, or someone who would stalk a victim through dark alleyways, or whether I would be a man of words, or even be transformed by the might of the divine into a woman like Saba whose moonlight-flooded curves I had pictured as my own.

My adolescence was full of possibilities, of becoming this or that, captive to ambition that changed with each night I spent in a different hut and listened to the hearts of those laying their heads next to mine, their breaths awakening gruesome thoughts as well as sensuous and compassionate ones. I am nothing but the sum of the many thoughts of those companions. Because, unbeknown to them, I became many things: an image of their generosity, a case study for their noble creeds, and a bearer of their most unbearable secrets.

Now here I am, I thought, awaiting Saba's trial while sitting among the good and bad, among those who committed their crimes and deeds in silence.

There was no police station here. Just us and our conscience. The unwritten law of silence, of family honour, of solidarity among the dispossessed and the kinship of inter-family marriages kept the camp plodding ahead on this path of purity, like a stream flowing between rocks and mountains, all the dirt receding at its depth. Even God has been fooled by us, a girl once said to Saba. That girl, who was dying during the labour of a baby conceived in rape, was not even fifteen.

But since God is of our making, we are only fooling ourselves, Saba replied.

As I looked around me, I realized why the judge had used my cinema instead of his own hut, which also functioned as a courtroom. The committee of elders had brought out the whole camp to witness the downfall of Saba.

My large compound was full. Every chair under the tree was taken. Boys perched on the compound's walls, like eagles, eyeing up the girls nestling on each other's laps. We have lived like this for a long time now, on top of each other, under each other's scrutiny. We policed, judged and imprisoned each other. How did Saba escape our gaze?

Babies crawled under the chairs, their lips still coated in their mother's milk. The ears of the only cat in the camp perked up. The heat freed odours from bodies crammed together. The clerk paced up and down the gallery with an incense burner. I leaned towards the aroma coiling in the air.

And when the clerk requested silence, declaring that the elders were about to come, I went around the gallery embracing my fellow rootless people, reaffirming my existence in their arms.

I hugged the rapist and raised the chin of his neighbour, a boy who still walked with bowed head. I thanked the molester and his wife for putting food in my mouth all those months ago and patted his bastard son and his daughter with whom I had shared a bed. I wondered whether the time was right to tell his daughter that after her father had finished with her, he came to me, and to ask her if she'd heard my muffled screams as I heard hers. No. Nothing like that. She and I shook hands. And I turned to the next silenced guilt. Here I was pleading with the adulterer not to forget to take my powdered milk after the trial to feed her malnourished children since she had poisoned her husband and ascribed his death to God. But in her sleep, I had heard her confess and console herself at the same time: I killed one bastard, but how many has God himself taken away from us?

A ll rise! yelled the court clerk.
The chatter gave way to the scuffle of a crowd getting to its feet. The judge arrived, accompanied by his three assistants.

My eyes turned away from the judge and peered through the screen, Cinema Silenzioso. Saba's name echoed around my compound. I wondered if people could see beyond the screen in front of which the clerk had placed a table and four chairs, and into Saba's compound. Saba was now sitting on her bed under the lime tree, her back to the court. Oil lamps flickered around her compound. She was not attending her own trial.

The judge stood to his feet and said nothing for a long time. He looked around the audience. His silent stares drew out gasps here and there. He lowered his head and broke down. His sobbing was so uncontrollable that he shook. He slumped in his chair.

The men making up the committee of elders shut their eyes. After sipping on water fetched by the clerk, the judge rose to his feet again. He drew a deep breath. His authoritative voice returned. Ladies and gentlemen, he said. It pains me to state that we have charged Saba with a grotesque sexual act against a hapless man. Her own disabled brother.

Silence. And then gasps that followed turned into shrieks when a woman in a white zuria walked to the front of the gallery and wept, throwing her arms in the air. As though she were a conductor, she had forced a familiar outpouring of collective grief. A young boy joined the raucous choir when he lamented, Why us? Why can we not live in peace?

I looked around me. Some bowed their heads and there were a few who turned side to side as if caught between belief and disbelief.

I noticed doubt in the eyes of those who blinked while muttering their disgust at Saba. Grief is beautiful when it is worn by people as a pretence. I felt this even more when a florid woman, with eyes that darted about to make sure she was being watched, fainted, and took down another woman and two men. One of them was the man who had raped me.

I was like a charcoal iron, smouldering inside. Birds resting on the shrubs inside my cinema flung themselves into the air and flocked above Saba's thatched roofs, heading towards the rugged hills.

The breeze blew and Saba's black dress hanging from the hibiscus tree on my screen shook. Her scent dispersed everywhere. I imagined her sadness too dispersing in the wind.

Saba abused Hagos. A woman cried as she beat her chest. Saba had abused poor Hagos. Our local doctor, the midwife, went around the court with a sliced onion to revive those who had fallen. The judge was on his feet again: Quiet. Quiet.

He composed himself. His hands no longer trembled. His back was straight. Mosquitoes buzzed behind him inside Cinema Silenzioso and around Saba's dress. The thirst for blood spilled outside when a man stood up and called for her head without a trial.

This trial must go on, the judge said.

The crowd quietened. His voice dropped. My brothers and sisters, he said. I have thought for weeks about whether it would be preferable to conduct this trial in private given the magnitude of the accusation, but I decided against it. We must establish the facts. Just how did this woman manage to take advantage of a poor man under our own eyes? We must learn lessons so this hideous crime will never happen again.

Silence.

The judge proceeded with the hearing. He called on his appointed court stenographer. And on came a thin young man, known around the camp for having a chest as deep as a well in the way he kept other people's secrets inside him. Yet he was light as a feather as he glided to the front of the gallery and sat on a chair to the right of the judge.

After registering Saba's full name, the judge, who insisted on pursuing correct court procedure from his Asmara days, asked the midwife if she knew Saba's age. The midwife, who had delivered Saba, couldn't remember. She gave some reference points of political events around the time of Saba's birth.

The judge ordered the appointed court stenographer to record her age as almost twenty.

It was as this point, when the stenographer took out of his bag a flat surface of wooden board used in the church and mosque to write verses from the holy book, that I volunteered to the court my own notebook.

To record facts about Saba, the stenographer leafed through a half-finished film script I had written about her, which I had intended to shoot when we returned to our free country. In my mind, as in my notebook, the real and imagined Saba coexisted side by side.

Saba's nationality, though, took longer to solve. Her mother was Ethiopian, said the midwife. But from what I can remember, I think her father was Eritrean.

I'll take your word, said the judge, as if eager to move on.

No, said a man. His eyes bulged as he added: If her father was Eritrean, then she is Eritrean. A child's identity follows that of the father.

The son of a slain fighter leapt to his feet. My mother didn't fight until she was martyred, he said, so that someone like you could claim that her identity mattered less.

The discussion raised a sarcastic laugh from a young man at the back of the gallery. He strode to the front waving his UN-provided identification. Look at this, he said. To me, to you, I am Eritrean, but, you see this here, this passport says I have no country. Why is that? Well? Well, why?

It was clear to me that he'd forgotten the point he was trying to make. So I snatched the ID out of his hand and announced to the public the intention I believed I had read in this man's smooth face. I think, I said to the gallery, this man is trying to remind us that since our country is still engaged in a war of independence, then, to the outside world, Saba's nationality is debatable.

Why? asked the man again.

I could hear muffled laughter coming from some in the audience.

I returned to my seat and looked at my cinema screen. Saba's compound was clear to see. She sat on her bed, a book in her hand. She was wearing her nightgown now. I had to look twice. I know about the peril of my cinema: sometimes when I recalled memories, they became so real, so alive on my screen. And I was full of memories of Saba.

Soon after, the court's proceedings were hindered once again, this time due to the lack of evidence regarding Saba's religion. Unconvinced by the varied accounts about her faith, that her father might have been a Muslim and her mother a Christian, the judge left a blank space. Religion unknown, said the judge to the stenographer.

A man stood up and wondered aloud: How is it that Saba has lived among us for all these years and yet we know so little about her?

The judge, who, in the absence of police authority in the camp, also had to act as an investigator, called the main witness.

In the far distance behind him Saba was still reading, and her compound basked in the yellow light of the oil lamps she had lined up against one of the walls.

The midwife sat on the witness chair. She took her oath and mumbled some prayers. The sorrow on her face vanished as she started her testimony.

I have been suspecting something was going on between Saba, may she be cursed, and Hagos since the afternoon, a few months after our arrival at the camp, when I entered their hut and found them lying together on a blanket. May the Lord forgive me for repeating this in front of you, Your Honour, but I discovered then that they had been sharing the same blanket ever since we arrived in the camp. I had to restrain myself from slapping that shameless girl. But no amount of beating was going to change her. I wished her mother had listened to me and had left her back home instead of paying so much money to bring her to this camp. You will never have peace with that girl, I had told her mother. I beg you, dear judge, to give her a severe punishment.

Please continue with your testimony and leave the sentencing to us, the judge said.

The midwife nodded. But she then turned towards us and, standing up, she wagged her finger as she addressed the fathers in the gallery. Be extra vigilant and extra forceful with your daughters. We are in a camp but a father is a girl's land and a girl would never be exiled from her culture and traditions with her father around.

Please could you sit down and continue, the judge said, shuffling in his chair.

As you wish, our judge, said the midwife. Anyway, I gave their mother my own blanket so her son would sleep away from that girl. I also know now why, when the businessman proposed to Saba, she immediately agreed without any of the trouble I had expected. I will never marry until I finish my studies, she used to tell her mother regularly. But when I brought the marriage proposal to her, she didn't even shed a single tear. All she asked in return, and in fact insisted on, was that her brother move in with them. It wasn't as if she was moving to a different village. But the kind-hearted and good-natured businessman agreed.

Yet, I was still blinded. How can I or anyone here accept that such a thing can take place in our community? I continued to hope it was all a misunderstanding. But my suspicions were heightened when, immediately after the marriage, Saba barred anyone from entering the compound. Even her own mother.

All these facts built up inside me, confusing me, but I never shared them with anyone. Except with the Lord. Then, a few months ago, their relationship was finally confirmed to me beyond doubt when Hagos was bitten by a snake in the middle of the night and the businessman came to seek my help. It had to take a near-death experience for them to open the gate of their compound to an outsider, and I never turn down a person in need. So I went, and to my horror, I found Hagos's hut full of women's clothes. Pants and bras in his bed. For all this time, Saba lived in his hut, and must have shared the bed with him.

The midwife finished and looked up, mumbling prayers.

The silence in the court continued.

I had watched Saba through the screen for so long, and now tried to remember if I had seen anything that aroused my suspicion. The judge called the next witness. He was known as the circumcised young man, even if we all are, because he was one of the few left with permanent disfigurement after the midwife cut him.

The young man with dishevelled hair, his shirt covered with straw and wet mud, waddled to the witness chair. I was convinced the judge had meticulously prepared his case to present Saba as a sexual predator, a woman who found satisfaction for her perversity in the extreme situation of human struggle. I had prayed then that he would not call on me to testify again. This was a man of law who learnt his trade at the hands of the British. A surprise, I assumed, lay around the corner.

The circumcised boy mumbled something no one could understand. For a street boy, he was shy. But then again, those who have lost everything seem most reluctant of letting go of what's inside them. The boy spoke in whispers, head bowed down. His voice opened up when he sat in the witness chair next to the judge, as if the responsibility and the attention of all the eyes focused on him freed his dying spirit.

Saba was his first lover, he said, and it was true you never forget the one who gave you your first orgasm.

The elders muttered their disapproval to the judge, but the man of law overruled their objection and instructed the young man to continue.

Sir, all I could remember after the midwife had done her job and washed the blood off the razor was Saba's face in the window. Then I fainted. It took me a few days after my circumcision to be able to stagger out of my bed, and the person who steadied me up as my knees buckled was Saba.

Stay in bed, she said to me.

I froze when I saw her. It was as if she had come to me in a dream. I touched her hand, felt her warmth. Where is my mother?

I told her to take a rest, Saba said. I am here now.

I didn't know you and my mother knew each other.

Saba smiled: We do now.

I want to get up, I said.

Saba held my arm and I could see how my hesitant steps, slow and agonizing like those of an old man, made her twitch, as if it was she who was in pain.

After faltering for a while, I said I wanted to take a piss. I had expected her to find a man to carry me to the open toilet, but instead she brought a large empty pot lying by the door and placed it at the centre of the hut.

And after helping me to hold on to the pole, she turned to leave. Wait, Saba. Can you help me with my robe? I can't bend.

I tensed my jaw, reclining my head backwards, biting my lips. My knees wobbled. Saba, I can't understand why my mother would need to circumcise me in this place.

Traditions go with us where we go, Saba said, as she raised the hem of my wide robe, red patches at its front. She didn't turn her face away as I expected her to. I shuffled and leaned my shoulder against hers. Long minutes passed and silence continued in the hut. Then, finally, I heard a drip on the tin. I squealed. And fell quiet again.

A warm breeze seeped inside the hut through the window. Her fluttering hair tickled my neck. Saba, please, lift my robe higher, you are hurting me.

I pushed once more. A few minutes passed and there was still nothing. I cried.

Don't worry, Saba said, wiping my eyes. I will help you.

It was like putting my burnt hand in cool water, like taking an aspirin. I grunted the moment she placed my wounded penis in her palm. The pain turned into a strange sensation the moment she pressed it. I couldn't stop crying. Then, in her blood-soaked hand, I noticed a trickle of white. Saba was my first love.

The judge stood up and shouted at the top of his voice to quell the commotion in the audience of the court. What kind of court is this where street boys' words are given credence?

Quiet. Quiet! The judge finally managed to stem the noise when he threatened to expel the whole crowd and continue the hearing in private.

Silence.

Mr Jamal, the judge called.

It was my turn to give testimony. The witness chair felt warm and sent a tingling sensation up my spine. I crossed my legs. I am ready, I said.

Very well, let's get to it then, the judge said. Please tell us everything you know about Saba. And let me remind you: anything you say will help us. We are interested in justice.

Let me start at the beginning, I said.

I first saw Saba at the river on our first evening in the camp when she jumped in the water after her brother to save a jerrycan that had been tugged from a woman's hand by the current. Job done, the brother and sister returned to their hut drenched, Saba carrying a bucket full of water on her head. I stood watching them, motionless and soaked through. Though I had hesitated to dive in the river to save Saba, I had lost my balance and fallen into the water.

I rushed back to the camp when I remembered the thick stack of birr notes I had hidden in a pocket sewn inside my underpants the night before fleeing home. I would have to spread the notes all over the floor of my hut to dry them. When I arrived back at the camp, I realized I didn't know where my hut was. Others returning from the river had their family members posted by their huts. Names were called out around me. But I had arrived at the camp alone. And I didn't leave a sign to enable me to identify my hut from the rest. I didn't even leave anything inside to reserve it as my own.

I opened one hut on my left and found at least five people lying on the floor close to each other, with white gabis covering their bodies. I jumped back, thinking death had already struck. But once I heard their deep breathing, I shut the door and tried the one next to it. This time, I avoided storming in. Instead, I pushed the door ajar and peered inside. An old man sat next to a woman and stared at the door with a watery secretion in his eyes. Have I woken you, Aboi? I asked.

No, my son, the old man said. Sleep is hard to come by these days.

I explained to him that I was looking for my hut. He said this was his and his wife's, but if I couldn't find mine, I was welcome to stay with them. There is no such thing as your hut or my hut, he said. Huts in this place belong to no one and to everyone.

I recognized the words often spoken by our fighters back home. Are you a Communist? I asked the old man.

I am sorry to disappoint you, son, but I am not educated. Compassion is something I learnt in my own village.

The couple in the adjacent hut were on their knees, praying. Heads bowed and eyes shut. They didn't even hear me open the door. The thought of people having taken my hut infuriated me. I took this anger with me to the next one. I kicked the door with my foot. A girl changing into her nightgown scampered to cover herself. I covered my eyes and shut the door. But as I passed the small window on the side of the hut, I stole a second glance. It was Saba, the girl who had saved the jerrycan with her brother at the river. I squatted under her window, facing the deserted square. At dawn, I turned and peeked through the window. Saba raised her knees. Her hands bypassed her inner thighs and instead opened her back cheeks. I wondered whether she was circumventing a wound or responding to a desire. Her body shivered. A moan escaped her mouth.

I remained seated as everyone around me yelled. I continued with my testimony, speaking in a loud voice that might be heard above the clamour.

After he brought his court to order, the judge asked me to continue.

I could see her.

See what, Mr Jamal?

I could see Saba standing in front of me.

Standing? Where? When?

In the open toilet, on the first evening we arrived in the camp. I couldn't warn her of my presence with a cough as the cold had damaged my vocal cords. And so, unaware of me, she put the torch on the ground. I saw the back of her legs, her purple thighs as she lifted her dress and crouched in front of me. I kept my eyes open as she picked up the stones, and when a beetle landed on her lower back, Saba jumped up and fled. I stumbled to my knees, parting the long grass with my trembling hands, sweat sweeping over my face, as if the heat emanating from Saba's spot in that field was the core of human warmth I have been searching for for a long time.

Uproar. He is telling lies. Throw him out.

Let me stop you there, the judge said to me.

But I continued: My Saba exists. Just look at the cinema and you will see her. You think that someone like the Saba I know can only be the creation of an insane man. As if real women are born from the ribs of men, and imaginary ones from their fantastical brains.

Enough of this, the judge said.

He ordered the guard to remove me from the witness chair. Turning to the midwife, he said, Please go to Saba and ask her to come to the court. This is her last chance. If she doesn't, we will send the clerk to drag her up here.

The court waited for the midwife. The judge was conversing with his fellow elders. Mutterings grew in the gallery. Rumours surfaced once again. I returned my attention to my cinema. Saba lay on her stomach, reading the book she now propped up against a pillow.

I looked away from Saba and faced the cage in which I kept pigeons by the side of my hut. The cat carefully balanced its feet like a ballerina on the thatched fence. Sometimes to confine is to prolong life, I thought to myself as I fixed my attention on Saba's compound.

Saba opened the door to the midwife. They talked. I could not hear anything in this silent movie I was watching. But I noticed their gesticulations, the way they cut the air with their hands. Saba turned in a circle. She threw her robe off and lay down on the bed.

I remembered that time, months before Saba's marriage, when, having suspected the worst after she saw Saba coming out of the Khwaja's hut at night, the midwife examined Saba's dignity. The midwife's two fingers in Saba's vagina confirmed her virginity then. That day, Saba's mother ululated as if the midwife had delivered her a new baby.

But why was the midwife checking Saba's virginity now, when she had been married to the businessman for months? I asked myself.

When the midwife rolled up her sleeve and approached Saba's opened legs with her two fingers, I was about to storm inside my cinema screen and run towards Saba's compound. The guard of the court halted my attempt to leave. Sit down. Sit down.

As I was pushed back on my chair, my eyes caught a glimpse of Saba sitting on her bed, head in her hands. Then, the gate of my compound was flung open. The midwife entered and ululated. Saba didn't abuse her brother. Saba is innocent, she said. Saba is a virgin.

Silence.

Those unbearable moments deafening in their stillness returned. It was only when a double-amputee ex-freedom fighter fired his Kalashnikov in the air that a collective scream of happiness erupted and shook the ground of my compound. Men pumped fists. Women ululated. And more people poured in through the gate of my cinema to join the impromptu festivities to celebrate Saba's rectitude and the camp's, which remained an island of purity in the middle of this bush. How our society kept its sanity even in this wilderness, said the judge, is a testament to our collective awareness. We police each other because we love others as much as ourselves.

The camp's singer mounted the judge's table. This camp has taken away many of us, taken a lot from us, but not our humanity, she sang. Saba hasn't stripped us of our humanity like war has stripped it from our homeland. We have nothing, except our honour. Thank you, shukor Saba. Thank you, pure Saba.

The singer held her krar close to her heart. I had never heard her sing in such a way. Now and then, her voice was drowned by the ululations, the claps of hands, the shouts of joy, the gasps of happiness.

The high notes of the krar brought more people to their feet, and as they went around the screen in a circle, in and out of Cinema Silenzioso, I recalled what Saba had said once, that our dance was conceived in response to our history, marred as it was by repetition of the same bloody story over and over again.

Saba was the woman who had dared to live by her own rules, who they would now bring back in line through a trial.

But no one had asked how it was possible that Saba was still a virgin after many months of marriage. Why hadn't she and her husband consummated their vows? Or, perhaps, everyone had known the answer, but had kept quiet in the hope that what was not uttered out loud lost its power to destabilize.

THE ARRIVAL

Tahir? Tahir, is this the camp?

The driver didn't answer. He squinted as he leaned forward. His chin rested on the steering wheel. The lorry veered and as he swerved to avoid a pothole, branches of an acacia tree scraped over the vehicle's side.

The driver sped up. Thick-kneed birds straggling over the slope of a hill scattered away. Saba looked at the sky above the birds' spotted wings. The sunset gathered intensity and traces of fading amber clouds blotched the horizon.

Saba searched for company in the side mirror. Dozens of lorries had set off at dawn from the city in which they had arrived while fleeing the war. Yet their lorry alone was on the road now. Her mother, sitting next to Saba, prayed. The same prayer she had been repeating since they had left home. Her brother, Hagos, sat at the back of the lorry, among the few belongings with which they had escaped.

My Lord, please brighten our way to safety.

Night fell over the sloping valley. The headlights of the lorry descending downhill dissolved the darkness. A flat surface dotted with huts glowed. But aren't refugee camps built with tents? Saba thought.

She was worried that if she blinked everything would be erased again. That the vastness of the journey that started on camels many days ago would return. Saba held on to the dashboard and focused on the image in front of her. But as Tahir swerved to avoid another pothole, the lorry hit a bump. The jolt threw the driver back into his seat and Saba grabbed the steering wheel. When it came down on the road, the vehicle jerked, and its light beams shifted from the cluster of huts to shrubland, and back again. Tahir braked.

We have arrived, Tahir said, fixing his turban. Saba, this is your camp.

Saba held her nose.

Dung.

Dung everywhere.

Tahir turned off the engine. The silence made the place feel more remote and deserted than she'd ever imagined. She looked up. There were no fighter planes, only a half moon that hung in the sky like the gold crescent ring her grandmother wore in her nose.

Saba examined the hut in front, which was illuminated by the lorry's lights. Her mother mumbled prayers and cried. Saba couldn't remember the last time she had seen her mother smiling or heard her laugh.

Tahir climbed down from the cabin and limped to the front of his lorry. As he opened the bonnet, smoke billowed out. Saba stepped out into the darkness. They were the first in the camp, she thought. There was no one else, not even an official to receive them. Saba wanted to ask Tahir about this when a flash of light from behind distracted her. She looked at the back of the lorry, where Hagos sat on jute sacks. His torch lit up a round hand-mirror which he was peering into, studying his face from every angle.

When Saba had wanted to pack her books, her mother refused. The smugglers demanded money for every extra bag, so while she managed to wear clothes in many layers, including underwear, she couldn't do the same with the books. So Saba stayed up days and nights before their departure, memorizing her favourite passages from the books she would leave behind.

And yet Hagos had brought that fragile thing the smugglers warned refugees against taking before they embarked on the camel journey.

Even people break on the road to safety, said the smugglers, let alone mirrors.

Hagos climbed down from the lorry into Saba's embrace. The scent of jasmine on his skin rose between them as she held him tighter. She pressed her hand into her brother's and looked at the round hut with its cone-shaped thatched roof. It was bordered by some shrubs. A moth rested on one shrub, the circles on its wings fluorescent in the lorry's headlights.

A distant hum grew into a growl that broke into a roar when one lorry after another pulled up into the camp. Noise erupted around Saba. Children shrieked. God was called upon. Ululations clashed with sobs. And as the lorries spread out and lit up various parts of the camp, the place glowed in fractions that looked like reflections of each other, one part duplicating itself here and there, clusters of huts casting shadows everywhere.

Saba watched as people disembarked from their lorries. Their shadows projected against the huts. Men and women like ants ferrying belongings on their backs and heads. Jute sacks. Clothes wrapped in scarves or gabis. Clay cooking-plate stoves. Children strapped to their mothers' backs. One man carried on the back of a woman, his legs around her waist, his arms wound around her neck. The woman panted as she trudged past Saba.

Before he drove away, Tahir took out a pen from his pocket. Hagos, he said, you remind me of myself when I was your age. I used to be silent too until I found a pen.

Hagos, though, didn't reach for the pen.

My son can't write, read or speak, their mother said.

Tahir looked at twenty-something Hagos. Is this true, Hagos?

Hagos stared ahead, away from Tahir.

Saba nodded. Yes, it's true.

Tahir left. And Saba already missed the smell of the lorry's cabin, the sun-baked fruits on the suede dashboard, dates that his parents harvested at the bend of the Nile. She missed the generosity that flowed from Tahir's hand. The same hand that gave her oranges, water, and gesticulated as he recalled his childhood memories under British rule, when he had to dip his tongue in cold water as if the only way to speak like the people of the North was to freeze his roots. He had also taken with him the way he spoke Arabic, in which every word stretched, each syllable extending its life on the tip of his tongue. In the camp, it would be rare to hear this accent again. Her thoughts darkened as more lorries departed.

Saba stared at the wooden door, its cracks visible in the light of their torch. Stench filtered through it. And darkness. Hagos held her hand as he pushed the door open. Her chest tightened. She turned around gasping for air. A nail protruding from the low door frame pulled out the pin holding her hair. Her sweaty locks tumbled down her face, concealing her eyes.

This is where we will live, said their mother, fastening her scarf around her waist to relieve the pain in her lower back, which had started to ache when the family of three started their journey hunched on a mattress tied on the camel's back.

Hagos gathered Saba's long, thick hair and tied it back into a bun. Saba followed him inside the hut that reeked of dung. He shone his torch around. Insects teemed out of the thatch. She watched the flight of a moth, its wings flapping in the heavy air. Hagos passed the torch on to Saba and went outside.

Saba contemplated the wooden pole made from a thin twisted tree in the middle of the hut. It went all the way to the apex, supporting the roof. She hoped she would not bump into it.

Hagos returned with jute sacks, his face bathed in the floodlight streaming from her hand. As he placed the sacks against the wall, Saba tried to compose herself too. They needed to make sure their mother could get some rest. Saba understood that when Hagos took out a blanket from one of the sacks. She followed his movements, wondering if she could ever care for their mother the way he did.

The thin blankets would be their sleeping pads, for now, their mother said.

Saba and Hagos held each end of a blanket. They beat it up in the air and laid it on the bare ground next to the wall, coughing in chorus.

Saba dusted off her black dress as Hagos helped their mother onto her blanket. Her bed. He folded a scarf into a pillow and placed it under his mother's head. He kissed her forehead and used his gabi, given to him at his cleanness party by the midwife who doubled as a circumciser, as a cover for his mother.

Saba spread out the other blanket on the opposite side of the hut. Here, Hagos and Saba would sleep. Share dreams. And a new life. This would be a place of reunion. They would spend nights talking. Laughing. Singing. Sharing stories from back home. And recounting childhood memories. Here, Saba would make up for the years she neglected Hagos. Years when she could see nothing around her apart from her textbooks. War had brought her closer to the person she had opened her eyes to first. Their mother often told her how, at only a few hours old, baby Saba had searched for milk on Hagos's chest. Hagos was also the first name she ever spoke. Hag. The other letters – o and s – came later. And like his name, his presence in her life would be realized piecemeal.

Saba peered through the window. She saw a group of men entering the square, their oil lamps flickering and their shadows merging into one amorphous body. Heavy and slow.

The group had gone out to search for the river. According to the lorry drivers, it should have been to the west of the camp. But they had turned back without success. There had only been bush.

We need to go back in the morning, said a man in a white jellabiya and black waistcoat. All we kept hearing was the hissing of snakes. We don't know what else is out there.

Scorpions. Antelope. Crocodiles. Elephants. Lions. Since Saba didn't know in which part of this country they were, she feared all its wildlife existed here. A camp in the middle of the bush.

The crowd swelled, reaching Saba's hut. Are you sure the river is to the west of the camp? asked a young boy with his baby brother swaddled to his back. Our driver said it was that way.

The boy pointed towards the opposite side from where the men had come. He was no more than twelve, Saba thought, watching him rock his brother. Please sleep, my sweet little brother. Please sleep.

The men, armed with sticks and oil lamps, split into four groups to venture out in all directions. Saba and Hagos joined the group led by an athletic-looking young man in a tracksuit.

The athlete, though, separated Saba's hand from Hagos's. This isn't an adventure for girls and women, he said.

Saba pushed past him, hooking her arm back around Hagos's. A hand pulled her back. Please let them go, said the boy with the crying baby. My little brother is thirsty.

The group of men left in search of the river. Saba stood still. Her eyes combed the dark border of the camp, which crept nearer as some oil lamps died out. Darkness brought thoughts in her head. What if a snake or a scorpion bit her brother? A crocodile swallowed him whole?

She unwrapped her scarf from around her shoulders. A warm breeze caressed her neck and enveloped her heaving chest, not giving it much reprieve. She was sweating.

Dots of light appeared to her left. A flickering glow of oil lamps bounced around as the men arriving from the west of the camp jumped and yelped. They had opened a route through the wilderness of grass, stones, shrubs and hills. The river is far, but at least we have water, said the athlete, his voice growing louder.

Saba was convinced it was Hagos who was the first to find the river. He wore a familiar look on his face, the pride of discovery, like when he had found an image of their grandmother being decorated by Emperor Haile Selassie. His sealed lips stretched wide and thin as he clenched his hand into a fist. But it was the athlete who reaped all the praise: You are a fearless lion. Because of you our children will not die of thirst.

Women ululated.

Saba hugged Hagos and wrapped her scarf around his shoulders. They walked back to their hut, fingers interlaced.

The camp set off to the river. Lamps and torches were held low, lighting up the ground, the habitat of dangerous creatures. The throng trampled over grass and shrubs and, as they filed through a pathway, the smell of foliage gave way to the scent of overripe cactus fruit. But soon the odour of human sweat overwhelmed the air.

Saba huddled up to Hagos. She clung to him, the fearless man whose bravery made sure that children, men and women would not die of thirst. She couldn't see his face, but knew he smiled at her whispering. As he always did.

Saba heard the river rippling, murmuring against the rocks. She breathed in fresh mud. The river must have flooded not long ago, she thought.

She stood as people placed their oil lamps on the ground behind them and lined up on the edge of the water. The river glistened between their legs, darkness enveloping the rest of the landscape. Saba clutched her yellow bucket to her chest, listening to containers clamouring and jerrycans hitting against each other. The silver bracelets of a woman in front of her tinkled as she dipped her jerrycan into the water. As the woman bent deeper, the bright colours of her adalkana dress bloomed around her hips like a rainbow against the pitch-black sky. The woman lost her grip and the river tugged away the jerrycan. Hagos scurried into the water. Lamps were lifted high and torches were directed at him. Why is he doing this? asked a man. Because the smallest of items have value now, said another. Hagos slipped. The river swallowed him, its shining golden layers swelling. Saba remembered the last time her brother had jumped into a flooding river back home to save a man who was escaping dergue soldiers. Facing up to danger was often his way of getting noticed. And Saba did what she always had done. She jumped in after him.

The brother and sister vanished underneath the water. It seemed an eternity before their heads surfaced again. Almost at the same time. And straight into the glow of the torchlight.

When Hagos stood in front of the woman, with the jerrycan returned and now filled with water, she placed her henna-clad hand on his shoulder. Thank you, the woman said. It was brave of you.

You are welcome, said Saba standing next to her brother. He is happy to help.

Back from the river, wet and shivering, Saba found her mother muttering to herself outside their hut.

How can you throw yourself in the water? she asked.

It wasn't dangerous, Saba said.

The danger was in the men's eyes.

I have survived bigger dangers, Mother, and you know it.

Do you know what Rahwa is saying about you now? The mother's voice broke. Her fingers trembled as she fumbled with her scarf.

The midwife is here? Saba turned away from her mother and kicked her foot in the air. Dust flew.

Saba was about to enter the hut when she noticed Hagos holding his mother's hands, kissing them into stillness.

God bless you, my sweet child, their mother said.

Hagos helped their mother inside the hut, while Saba watched from the door, still in her soaked black dress. Hagos sat by their mother's side, massaging her arms. Saba went behind the hut to change into her nightgown. The torch she placed on the ground made an eerie glow on the hut opposite. She noticed that the door stood open. A foot emerged in the fringes of the torchlight, which curled around an ankle. I can be seen everywhere, Saba thought. Inside and outside.

She retreated inside the hut. Hagos rolled himself to one side of the blanket. Saba stepped over her brother and squeezed herself in the tiny space next to the wall made of dung. They lay down so that her face was next to his feet. Small stones pierced the thin blanket. Saba spooned herself between the curved wall and a curled-up Hagos.

THE MOSQUE IN THE SAND

It was dark when Saba lay on the blanket with her eyes shut. She touched herself in the way she always did back home in the moments before dawn when her body belonged to her.

But that first morning in the camp, when her chest swelled above the ground like a taut dewdrop on a leaf, she heard their mother grunt in her sleep. The moan of pleasure died behind Saba's clenched teeth. She sat up and shuffled away from Hagos. A twig protruding out of the mud wall grazed against her leg. She pounded the wall with her fist.

Back home, her room had opened onto the garden of a stone-floored courtyard with terracotta pots full of herbs. She had inherited that room from her grandmother. It was here that Saba's grandmother found a way to communicate her desire for her neighbour by planting flowers against the wall separating them. Although her trader grandmother grew up without parents, she taught herself to read and write, founded a business before she turned twenty, and travelled from one country to another, from one lover to the next. Her longevity owed itself to tej wine, khat and sex.

Apart from the photo of her grandmother, which Saba had hung on the wall above her bed, that room was decorated with pictures she had hand-picked from the studio of their landlord, where her mother worked as a servant. The landlord, who had gone to Europe as a student carrying his hometown's dreams, but returned having fulfilled only his own – to qualify from an art school – had appointed himself as Saba and Hagos's godfather. One of the photos Saba had taken from his studio was of a girl with a Kalashnikov slung over her shoulder. Suspended behind the freedom fighter, through the photographer's trickery, Saba could see the central avenue in Asmara that had changed names three times in recent memory, from Mussolini Avenue, to Queen Victoria Avenue, to Emperor Haile Selassie Avenue, and now the National Avenue under the dergue. The fighter, though, stood against the conquerable street as firm and rooted as the palm trees on both sides of the grand boulevard. Saba practised this pose, to replicate it in her border town.

Next to the fighter there was a copy of a painting given to her by the landlord. The pale skin of a nude woman taking a bath somewhere in Paris still glowed when Saba dimmed the light to sleep.

Books covered the floor and Saba's bed. History in Tigrinya, translated Russian novels in Amharic, poetry in Arabic. Pencils. Pens. Erasers. Politics. Art. Freedom. Africa. Europe. And Saba. All vying for a space in her small, disordered room.

The realization of where she was now shook her out of her reverie. Saba buried her face in her hands, feeling the density of the mud walls around her. She sat on her knees. The earthy smell of shrubs under her window rose and mixed with the dung-smothered morning air. She raised her fingers to her face and inhaled the scent of her thighs.

Saba staggered out of the hut. Streaks of orange light appeared on the horizon, as curved as the humps of a camel. Footsteps shuffled across the sandy ground. A figure emerged from a narrow passage into the square. The man stopped in the middle of the square, placing the oil lamp he was carrying on the ground next to him and creating a circle of radiance around his feet. He announced the call to the first prayer of the day.

No one answered. The man waited, arms folded. Dust covered his sandals. Without his turban, his gabi, his rug, without a minaret, a dome, four walls, a direction of prayer, the imam's authority, Saba thought, was left in the lean and tall silhouette of his shadow printed on the bare ground of the camp.

He called for the prayer again and again. His voice grew hoarse. No response. He soon fell silent. He dug his foot in the sand and dragged it along, beginning to outline a place of worship. He stopped and looked back. The faint outline behind him grew dimmer as he marched onwards with his oil lamp. He returned to the starting point and began all over again. A hardened fighter refusing to give up a battle despite losing his armoury. That thought came to Saba as she walked towards him, and followed his outline, digging her foot harder and deeper behind him, marking human presence in this wilderness.

The imam lifted his lamp. Her face glowed in response to his smile. He coughed. He regained his voice.

This should be big enough, he said after a while. But we can expand it if needed. After all, it is a line in the sand.

Where is the direction of prayer? Saba asked.

The imam raised the hand with the oil lamp high against the sky. Rays of light poured from his high arm. God is everywhere, he said.

The mosque in the sand was completed. Saba skipped back to her hut as if she had participated in the construction of a real mosque that would last beyond her life on earth. The thought, though, made her shiver. What if life in the camp ended up being only as firm as that line in the sand?

The imam prayed alone. His jellabiya fluttered in the breeze, the white fabric pressed against the darkness. Saba picked up her torch and set out to search for a school in the camp. When her mother had decided to flee with her children, Saba had asked if there was a school on the other side of the border. Saba's mother threw a shoe at her daughter. Our neighbours have been killed, she said. We are leaving home, and all you think about is school.

Saba's cousin, who came to bid them farewell, took her aside. You need to be patient and find the right time for your questions. But don't worry, you are going to the biggest country in Africa. And it is full of educated and intelligent people.

Even the war would not interrupt Saba's march towards her dream then. Only divert it. Like the Nile, it would face hills, mountains, forests, and find a way to pass through many countries.

The alleyways were a labyrinth in which she could get lost. Saba continued, diving into the dark. She stumbled upon unused thatch scattered alongside woods, twigs, ropes. The builders of the camp must have left in a hurry, she thought. She stepped over the abandoned litter on the ground and turned left into another lane. Doors were shut. The familiar sounds of morning were absent. There were no cockerels to announce the arrival of dawn. There was no scent of roasted coffee beans in the air. Air untouched by berbere mixed with ghee, by aftershave, by perfumes. Saba walked on enveloped by a different kind of morning that lacked the rhythm of dough slapping against mogogo stoves, of spoons clinking against pots as women stirred flour to make ga'at porridge. She didn't hear car engines sputtering. Bicycles clicking in the hills. The place was empty of women and men rushing to the fields, to the market, of students reading aloud from their textbooks. This was a silent morning.

And where is the school? Saba asked herself, shining her torch higher, lighting up the yellow pointy roofs that stabbed the dark skyline. As if a school could be up there, a castle above the clouds.

It was as she leaned against her hut that the sun dispersed the remnants of the night. Saba noticed a young man wearing a yellow flat cap staring at her, his head tilted to the side, his mouth open. She wondered if he was mistaking her for someone he'd left behind or someone killed in the war. The sun intensified. Heat rose off the ground into the skirt of her black dress. Her preference for black clothes went back to the time she had suffered burns to her thighs, turning her skin purple. Saba wore black to remind herself of what she loved and had lost forever.

Good morning, said the young man. My name is Jamal.

Saba didn't respond.

Panting, Jamal swung round to face the square. There is no shop in this camp, he said. There is nothing. Nothing. Nothing.

Calm down, said another man, striding past Saba.

Saba pushed herself to her feet and stared at this light-skinned man with narrow shoulders and slick black hair, in a blue cardigan over a blue shirt, blue trousers and shiny black shoes. He had a book, its title written in English, under his arm.

The man bowed his head at Saba and, patting Jamal on the back, he said, Remember, it is the absence of things that makes people creative. Things will change.

How? said Jamal. Have you looked at this place? Maybe you need to wear your glasses.

The man removed his glasses from his head and put them on. What a glorious sun, he said. I feel it is going to be a wonderful day.

This is Africa, Jamal said. The sun is always bright and so it was on the day the war came to us. Weather has nothing to do with how great one's day is going to turn out.

The man chuckled, his shoulders shaking. The book under his arm nearly slipped out, but he caught it before it hit the ground.

Do you have a pen and paper, Khwaja? said Jamal. I need to write my film script.

Need is no longer a word appropriate for this place, the man said, without objecting to Jamal using the nickname for a Westerner for him. Yes, I have a pen, but I'd rather keep it. After all, you are right, there is no shop in this camp.

I think I saw you in Cinema Impero when I worked there, said Jamal.

Perhaps, the Khwaja said, laughing. I am glad to meet a fellow Asmarino in a refugee camp. The world is small, they say.

The Khwaja slipped his hands into his pockets and smiled at Saba. Buongiorno, shokorina, he said. Che bella giornata.

And he sauntered off, greeting those on his way in various languages, even those brought by the colonizers. Saba wondered whether his peace with himself was because the conflicts in his mixed blood were in the past. But for Eritrean-Ethiopian Saba, half from an occupied country and the other half from the occupying, the conflict was ongoing. Half of her was at war with the other half. That's why she was in a camp.

Saba left Jamal and followed the Khwaja through the camp. His blue outfit reminded her of what her father had worn the morning he carried her to school to take Hagos's place, when Hagos was pulled from school by their parents after a visiting doctor diagnosed him as mute. That day, Saba saw Hagos hiding behind a tree outside the school. She waved at him. Hagos ran away crying.

Saba trailed the Khwaja as he made his way through the crowd, swerving around people, saying sorry, scusami, pardon me, a'thazouli, asmhoelee. He stopped in front of a group of men huddled over a torn newspaper, words hanging low to the ground. A man cut the paper into pieces as if it was a loaf of bread and divided it among his companions. The men scattered off in different directions with broken sentences, as if nothing needed to make sense.

Music bellowed out. A singer tuned her krar. The high-pitched beat drew people. From now on, the singer said in her honeyed voice, she would only sing about the war to make sure no one forgot why they were here. Her nephew, though, whispered to Saba and those nearest to him that he was carrying memories of all her love songs as well as of the beats of his double-headed drum. He promised to heat the blood of the dispossessed with one side of the koboro and soothe the hearts of lovers with the other.

Further up the square, a widow had dressed up for her first outing in the camp. She wore a green dress with sequins sewn to its wide lush hem. She had consigned her mourning dress to the bottom of her jute sack, she said to those around her. A woman mourns, but a woman moves on too. The Khwaja patted the widow's back. Saba noticed the mark of his dusty hand on the young woman's green dress.

An eagle circled the camp. The bird threw its shadow on a girl painting her toes as her mother began to set her hair in rollers. The girl's name passed from one boy's lips to another. Samhiya. From Asmara. Samhiya popped her chewing gum and, placing her red lips on her palm, she blew kisses to those in front of her. Her cherry-flavoured breath wafted over to Saba.

When she turned away from the city girl, Saba saw the woman whose jerrycan her brother had saved the night before. The woman wandered into the square, wearing a long yellow gown. The adults, including Saba's mother, were searching for familiar faces in the crowd. But some faces must have changed, Saba thought. Or were, at least for now, masked with sorrow. Her mother had not been the same since the camel took its first step away from their hometown. Saba wondered if she herself had changed too.

Strangers consoled each other, fighting back grief with small talk to shore up strength, and in doing so they established new friendships. The Khwaja, though, joined the children running around, laughing, falling and crying along with them.

As Saba looked at the scenes unfolding in front of her, it occurred to her that life in this place would be about searching for alternatives. Hopes and prayers murmured in the square caused a silent tremor across the camp. Right under her feet.

Saba came out of her hut clutching a handful of seeds from an orange that Tahir had told her to plant. They will grow into a beautiful orange tree, he said.

A gust of wind blew through the camp. Doors flapped. Rope latches snapped. A cloud of dust swirled around Saba. She closed her eyes. Screams echoed through the square, then faded. And when the wind calmed, Saba looked further down the square. The mosque that she had helped build in the sand was erased. She looked at the seeds in her hand. Was there any point in planting them?

A few yards away, a priest in a white turban, a white gabi draped over his white tunic and white pants, stood head bowed as if in prayer. Flies crawled on his shoulders. He raised his horsehair fly swatter and uttered prayers to the congregation standing in a circle around him, some huddled close as children do to a mother.

Saba tried to guess the time by observing the sun's position in the sky. Light flooded her retinas until the sun's glare forced her to cast her gaze away from the sun, from time.

Squatting low, she dug a hole in the ground close to the wall of her hut with her bare hands. A girl sneaked up on her and asked what she was planting.

I love oranges, said the girl, introducing herself as Zahra. I will help you, this hole is not deep enough. We also need to surround the hole with sticks and logs so that people don't walk over the seeds. We have to look after this, I can't believe we are doing this already.

Saba gaped at her.

Zahra's laughter drew Hagos out of the hut.

Am I talking sense?

Saba nodded, her eyes lingering on Zahra's face.

Ah, this, Zahra said, rubbing the scar on the bridge of her nose. I fell off the camel on the way to this country. We all have wounds, but some are just more visible than others.

Saba uncrossed her legs and pulled up the hem of her dress, settling it around her purple thighs.

Was that a bomb?

No, said Saba.

Those who love you most are also most capable of hurting you, Zahra said.

Saba said nothing. She forced her eyes away from Zahra, towards where the smoke wafted in the distance, towards the eagle that steered its way between thatched roofs, and towards the blue sky.

Saba!

Saba shuddered when Zahra pulled her in for a tight embrace. I am sorry, said Zahra. I didn't mean to remind you.

Silence.

Thank you, said Saba.

Saba gave her new friend – in her mind, friendship was already exchanged – some of her seeds.

They started planting. This will be a beautiful orange tree, said Zahra.

But it doesn't mean that just because you are helping me now it's going to be our tree, said Saba, laughing.

It takes more than twenty years for these seeds to grow into an orange tree, said Zahra. By then I hope none of us will be in this place.

Saba kept digging.

Saba, say amen, said Zahra.

Double amen, said Saba, chuckling.

Zahra had come to the camp with her grandmother. Her mother had stayed back in the trenches, fighting the independence war.

But we will be back home soon, Zahra said to Saba. That's what my mother promised me.

What is your mother's name? she asked.

Major Lemlem, said Zahra, her voice rising as if she could no longer hold on to this secret.

Major Lemlem, Saba repeated as she looked at Zahra.

Soon after the two girls began planting the seeds, Samhiya arrived, hair set in red rollers, trailed by boys.

My God, Saba, Samhiya said. Who taught you to swim like a boy? And by the way, everyone in the camp knows your name after last night.

Saba had forgotten about her dive into the dark water. She straightened her back and pointed at Hagos, who was standing by the door. My brother taught me, Saba said. He is the best.

Samhiya craned her head towards Hagos.

Are you sure you are a man? I mean you are so beautiful, that's what I meant, she stammered, breaking into a giggle.

The boys behind Samhiya sniggered.

The look on Hagos's face didn't change. Saba had long understood his silence was like a pair of dark glasses on a blind man. But she hoped he would at least respond to his admirer with an expression.

Let her see your even more beautiful smile, Saba mumbled at him.

Would you teach me, please? Samhiya asked Hagos.

Saba's grin widened until it pierced the dimples on her cheeks. A chance of affection had arrived in Hagos's life, she thought. Finally.

Hagos's eyes, though, were fixed on his sister. Saba reached with her hand to his face as if to turn him towards Samhiya. She stopped. Yes, Saba said to Samhiya. Hagos will be happy to teach you to swim.

Samhiya rolled her head back and asked Saba, Why can't he talk for himself? Did I make him speechless?

He is mute, said one of the boys behind Samhiya.

Silence.

Saba abhorred those moments when girls became quiet, perhaps pondering life with a handsome but disabled man.

I have to go, said Samhiya, planting a kiss on Saba's cheek. Ciao bella.

Saba brushed past Hagos and barged inside the hut. Her brother followed her, closing the door on those left outside.

THE EXPIRED SARDINES

A convoy of lorries, led by a Land Rover, unzipped the crowd as it rumbled into the square. Oil dripped, turning the ground darker in parts. Saba squinted against the sun and was only able to make out the sight of men in jellabiyas huddled together on top of brown jute sacks in the back of the lorries. An eagle flew above them, its black wings spread against the blue sky. The Land Rover and the lorries stopped opposite three huts with blue doors grouped around a low cement building.

Saba advanced towards the newcomers with Zahra and her grandmother. Two passengers came out from the Land Rover, a white man and a light-skinned Habesha-looking man. They entered one of the three huts making up the aid centre and shut the door.

Let us through. We need to talk to the aid workers.

Saba turned behind her. Three men with white hair, gabis wrapped around their shoulders, pressed through the throng. I am a senior judge in Asmara high court, said one of the men to the implacable crowd, he was tall with trimmed beard and wide eyes.

Oh yeah, said the athlete, and I am the mayor of Asmara.

The so-called judge smiled. It is good to see we never lose our sense of humour, he said. You are right: anyone in a camp could claim to have been anything back home. When the dergue evicted me, they burnt all my documents. But I carry my history in my blood.

The crowd applauded.

The judge – Saba believed him – nodded at the crowd, and said, I don't have any proof. God, the greatest, is my witness, but I can also debate law and order as I studied it during the British rule of our country.

We are lucky to have such a learned and God-fearing man among us.

Saba recognized the midwife's shrill blurting from behind. She didn't look back.

The time is right to set up a qebele, said the midwife, pushing her way between Saba and Zahra to shake the judge's hand.

What is a qebele? Saba whispered to Zahra's grandmother.

Don't whisper, ask them, loudly, said the grandmother.

Saba grinned at the theatrics of Zahra's grandmother when the grandmother suggested that Zahra carry Saba on her shoulders so that her question would be heard by many.

Hesitating, Saba got on Zahra's back and shouted: What is a qebele?

Heads turned towards them. Well, said the grandmother, now that she had caught the full attention of the crowd, this is a tradition that allows only men to rule us. God willing, it will be destroyed when our country is free.

Saba looked on amazed as the grandmother walked away head held high.

Soon after, the aid workers emerged from their makeshift offices. The white man, said to be an English aid coordinator, put up a signpost by the huts. The prospect of discovering a name for this place in the wilderness stirred Saba. Standing on her toes, she peered over shoulders at the sign in blue bold letters. It was the same two words in three languages. Refugee Camp, it read in Tigrinya, Arabic and English.

The elders shook the aid workers' hands and, turning to the crowd, the judge called for a prayer. May God bless their work, the square prayed.

Food allocations were handed out from the lorries. Each family received coupons according to its size. The first morning only tins of sardines were available. The rest – maize, oil, milk powder and sugar – was on its way, so explained the aid coordinator to the people via his assistant who doubled as a translator.

People forged into the square from every direction. Saba had never seen such a wide variety of people in one place. Some had lighter skin, others dark features, the thin walked alongside those with bellies. Faces were different in more than expression alone – here were incised cheeks, and there were noses with crescent rings, eyebrows pierced, crosses tattooed on foreheads, hair braided with shells, beards dyed with henna.

There was so much to take in. Too many dialects and idioms she couldn't understand. What glued her country together was more than one language or one religion, and Saba wondered if she could find it in this camp. She was pushed from one tribe to another. Her breathing became heavy. Yet, she drifted along as if she was on a journey, travelling across her country, visiting tribes she had only ever read about, encountering people who occupied different corners of a nation all in the same place. At the same time. Was it possible for a whole country to have evacuated to a camp? Was it possible for a land bombed day and night to seek rest elsewhere, along with all its inhabitants?

Saba and Zahra filed past mothers who tied their babies on their backs with their embroidered zurias, mothers who rocked in harmony and hummed in unison.

A woman with a cross tattooed on her forehead sat on a man's shoulders, her arms spread wide open calling for her missing daughter. But everyone is lost, Saba thought, as people strayed into each other's path, separating one another.

In the middle of all this chaos, there was a long queue. Like a stream running through wild rocks. The English queue, the Khwaja had called it.

When Saba joined the queue with Zahra a hot, dry wind blew in from the river, carrying with it the smell of the open toilet mixed with the wild flowers in the hills. The air made Saba feel hot and nauseated.

The queue came to a halt. Zahra hummed a melody.

What is that song? Saba asked.

My mother used to tape herself singing to me, Zahra said.

It's a beautiful melody, Saba said, and bowed her head as if heavy with memories of all her battles with her own mother.

That is what mothers do when they are away from you. They sing to you through a tape to make up for their absence.

Can you sing it for me? asked Saba.

Yes, Zahra nodded, smiling and squeezing Saba's hand:

My Zahra, I miss you,
The few hours I am at the base,
I think about nothing but you,
The time I breastfed you, washed you, made your food, sang for you
    at bedtime,
But I return to the trenches
Full of determination, and I fire my gun as though you are strapped to
    my back,
Whispering in my ear
To hurry, to keep going, and reminding me that I am here,
I am here to bring back my country,
Where my daughter will have the same rights as someone else's son.

Carrying rocks across the fish-stinking square, the imam and his fellow worshippers trudged past Saba and began outlining the boundaries of a new mosque.

Saba was on her way home from the aid centre, the image of Zahra's fighter mother etched in her mind, when she encountered the Khwaja. He was talking to a group of turbaned men seated on the ground around an opened tin of sardines. Eyes shut, faces grimacing.

I can't eat this, said one of the men with a piece of fish dangling in front of his scrunched-up nose.

I have never seen your hand shake so much, said his younger companion. Even when you used to slaughter a cow. Swallow it and God will ease it through your throat.

The man swallowed.

His companions were about to clap when the man spat out the fish and his sea-smelling words: I lived in the Sahel all my life and never touched fish. Can someone go and tell the Englishman not to impose his cuisine on us?

Saba laughed.

Actually, the Khwaja said, by eating fish we are showing our ability to adapt, and like a tall building, our new free country will be flexible to withstand nature's challenges as it rises on our backs.

He pulled his book from under his arm and turned to a thumbed page, reading an English poem he translated as he read:

> *If you can make one heap of all your winnings*
> *And risk it on one turn of pitch-and-toss,*
> *And lose, and start again at your beginnings*
> *And never breathe a word about your loss;*
> *If you can force your heart and nerve and sinew*
> *To serve your turn long after they are gone,*
> *And so hold on when there is nothing in you*
> *Except the Will which says to them: 'Hold on!'*

As Saba angled her head to check out the title on the cover, the Khwaja closed the book and moved. Saba followed him. He stopped in front of another group. Here, a mother was struggling to feed her child. The baby ducked under the spoon his mother tried to put into his mouth. I lost all my milk on the day of the bombardment, the baby's mother said when the Khwaja asked her why she couldn't breastfeed him instead.

As the mother scooped another spoon of mashed sardine, Saba spotted the date printed on the side of the tin. This tin is out of date, she mumbled to herself.

Back in the hut, Saba put the tin on the ground and examined the Arabic writing on the side. Taking a small piece of wood from the floor, she scratched over the expiry date. The black letters dissolved. Time no longer matters, she thought.

As she turned around, she bumped into the pole in the middle of the hut. She held it with both hands and looked up. Everything was as it had been when she left that morning. She sat on the blanket and thought of their brick house back home. Four rooms, a shower, a latrine and a courtyard with trees and flowers. Now home had been reduced to this round single space. A town to this camp. A country to this wilderness. Saba, the student with a plan, to a refugee.

A beetle dropped at her feet from the roof. It was covered in dust and limped slowly forward. Saba wondered what else lived in the tree branches that rested on the mud wall and the central pole, around which the thatch was tied with ropes. She had bent down to scoop up mounds of dirt from the floor with her hand when Hagos came in with a bundle of long grass. He tied the stalks together with a rope to make a broom. As he bent to sweep the floor, the thin sunbeams seeping through the tiny window played across his face.

People noticed Hagos's looks. Some even remarked they could see God's fairness in his perfect features. God took, but also gave. Saba stood still to admire this work of divine compensation. She followed him with her eyes as he flitted across the hut with his broom. Behind him, dust coiled in the sunlight.

Every woman, her grandmother told her once, carries an ideal man in her heart, someone who made the challenges of being born a girl a little bit easier. Hagos was that man for Saba. They linked each other's worlds. He carried out domestic chores, bought her clothes and shoes, took care of her hair, all while she focused on her studies.

But she too sacrificed something for Hagos. She allowed herself to be turned into the woman he carried within him. She could see it in the way he dressed her, styled her hair, trimmed her nails, painted her fingernails.

They were a match, he and she the other of the other.

When Hagos straightened up, Saba approached him and blew the dust off his face. He seemed to her as if he had been sculpted out of a smooth rock. His wide eyes appeared like the sea in which she dived to search for the words he might have wanted to say but couldn't. Saba was his confidante, his sole friend. She had first realized this many years ago. She had just returned home from the hospital where she had undergone treatment for the burn injuries to her thighs, when Hagos barged into her room. Usually, he would knock before entering her room and she would have time to clear her bed of books, hide the words, the equations, the science and history taken away from him when his parents pulled him out of school and instead invested whatever money they had in her.

That evening, though, Saba froze. She looked at him and then down at her books. Hagos sat on her bed holding her face in his hands. Their eyes met. Hagos was talking to her. The deeper she looked into his eyes, the more she felt she could interpret his feelings spread on the surface, and condense the thoughts and possibilities going through his head into something that made sense.

I understand you, Hagos. I am not imagining this. It's real. I can see in your eyes what you are trying to tell me.

Hagos burst out crying. Saba cried with him.

Now Saba placed the broom against the wall and hugged her brother, as if he was a precious discovery she had just made. Hagos stooped a little, allowing his slender body to be enveloped. He sighed and muttered. His lips tickled her earlobe. I love you too, she whispered back.

Hagos took a bristle brush out of his jute sack and straightened his sister's naturally curly hair, though she liked it as it was. She tilted her head back as he arranged a red bandana to keep her hair away from her face. She had never told him she detested that colour. As he put earrings on her ears, she grimaced in anticipation of the itching she'd feel in reaction to the silver, and allowed him then to add a short heart-shaped necklace. He turned her into a cliché, she thought, as she coughed when he sprayed her neck with a perfume he made from ingredients he picked up at the market back home. But then again, Saba thought, that which is cliché for many is original for someone as isolated and lonely as Hagos.

Hagos turned around as Saba squeezed into the black underwear he had tailored at their uncle's shop to replace the skin she lost in the fire started by the midwife. Saba withstood Hagos's preparations before they left for an early-morning walk in the camp. Though she owned her mind, she had given her body to Hagos a long time ago. It made sense. She had taken his place in school and it was fair to give him this alternative form of self-expression. He used her skin in his way, to write his story.

Saba and Hagos navigated the crowded square. Voices mingled into raucous, incomprehensible noise. Their walk was interrupted by a man searching for aspirin, by a young girl who whispered in Saba's ear, asking for cotton wool for her first menstruation, and by the athlete who was looking for men to donate their socks to make a large sock ball. Hagos doesn't wear socks, Saba said on her brother's behalf. Adding, Go to hell, when the athlete replied that he pitied a man when a woman became his voice.

When they arrived at the other side of the square, they encountered the midwife reviving a man who had fainted by holding a slice of onion under his nose. Hagos turned Saba's head away from the green-eyed woman. But looking away didn't amount to forgetting, Saba thought. Not when her thighs still bore marks of the midwife's cruelty.

Passing a hill with a solitary hut to the east, Saba and Hagos arrived outside the camp. They climbed one of the surrounding hills. Saba inhaled the scent of wild jasmine and hibiscus trees scattered about them.

Saba couldn't see the river but knew its muddy water flowed behind the broad hill to the right. More hills poked out of the earth and clipped the horizon with their patches of red and grey rocks. The valley was strewn with pebbles and stones. The long grass of the open toilet in front of them swayed in the wind, the breeze carrying the foul odour.

Saba surveyed the camp nested in the folds of the valley behind the open field. The sparsity of their new home sharpened under the morning sun. There is nothing in this place, Saba said, echoing Jamal's words. Nothing. Nothing. Yet, as she bemoaned the absence of school, calmness ran through her. For once, she would be able to live without fighting with her mother and the midwife, without the permanent guilt towards Hagos. In fact, she thought, she could teach him all she knew, if he allowed her to, and they would spend the rest of their lives with this limited shared knowledge. Neither of them better than the other. Saba placed her head on Hagos's shoulder and closed her eyes to the light.

The chirping of crickets drifted in through the window. Saba sat up on her blanket and crawled over to the other side. She shook Hagos's shoulder.

Hagos? Hagos, can you hear me?

Silence.

Hagos, I can't sleep. My stomach hurts.

Silence.

Does it feel like it has been weeks already to you too?

Silence.

But maybe it has. Do you know how long we've been here?

Silence.

Saba stretched alongside Hagos. His breath warmed her face. Beads of sweat covered her forehead.

Silence.

Leaving her brother to sleep, Saba shuffled out of the hut. Dawn reddening the thatched roofs with a rosy hue. Birds chirping. The faint cries of babies. The call to prayer. Footsteps. Flip-flops. Bare feet dragging through sand. Men. Yawning. Greeting each other. Salaam. Sabah al-kheir. Dhan hadeerkum. O Jesus our Saviour. A priest. Clay incense burner in his hand. Charcoal burning into the pores of dawn. Incense rising. Saba walked through the haze of incense smoke, head down, arms folded.

She entered the open toilet, listened for a cough, the customary decorum of a shared toilet. The person first there alerted the incomer of their presence. There was no one. She crouched. Then, a jet of water splashed against the grass behind her. Saba leapt to her feet and ran away.

THE OPEN TOILET

Saba shuffled on her stool next to the open furnace. She wanted to ask her mother just how long they had been here. Days? Weeks? She could see time passing on her own body, on the people around her. People in the square had said this was a temporary place and the day of return would not be far off. For now, though, life itself was suspended, quietly churning like milk in a goatskin. Soon it would curdle.

The family of three sat down in a circle on the round thatched rug Hagos had woven together days before. In the middle of this gathering were a jerrycan, a tin of sardines, tea made from the black powder which Saba had bartered from a neighbour in exchange for sugar, and himbasha bread which their mother had baked before leaving their hometown and rationed ever since. It had hardened, but water dissolves even mountains, said their mother, as she sprinkled it over the bread, mumbling prayers.

The hut smelt of fish. Saba closed her nostrils. Eat, the mother said. You are losing weight.

But no matter how big she was, Saba thought, she would never fill her mother's eyes.

Eat, the mother said. Eat.

You are like a little girl, the mother said. Eat. Here, take some of my food.

Saba looked at her mother, who had paid for her daughter's schooling by working as a servant. Saba now had to come up with something else to compensate for all her mother's hard work. She needed to put on weight, Saba thought, to offer something tangible to sell to men. Saba stared at her mother's hand. Her three fingers – the thumb and the middle and index fingers that made an elegant hand-spoon for a lady – held a small piece of bread. The food in her hand was barely visible. It was a skill Saba had failed to inherit. The invisibility that a woman ought to inhabit. Saba was heard and seen. She argued. Talked. Laughed. She left traces of her presence everywhere. At home, for not being girl-like. At school, for being the best. Even at the market, where she fought back. Once she'd squeezed a man's bottom, to repay the compliment, she said. The man, an off-duty policeman steeped in tradition, slapped Saba for stooping so low, and for turning, he said, our culture on its head.

The faint light seeped through the window of the hut. Behind her mother, she saw slippers, a plastic stool, the open furnace. Next to pots and cups, there were the jute sacks, where they kept their clothes. They had exchanged vows not to look into each other's sack, as if they were locked, keys deposited with their respective owners.

A puff of dust flew in through the window. Hagos stood up and closed the beaded straw curtain he had woven himself.

Her mother's eyes were red. Women, her mother said, were the colanders through which the suffering of their nation was purged. But Saba wondered how much she herself had contributed to her mother's sadness. Their mother had been hurt by having a mute child and two dead infants. Saba's father said he couldn't live with the continuous wailing, her inability to accept fate. Saba's mother lived her life waiting for the next misfortune to strike. He wanted to be with a woman who could love. He was gone by the time Saba turned six.

According to the midwife, though, Saba was the main source of her mother's anguish. The mother had imagined a life with a daughter who would be by her side, learning from her, listening to her, relieving her duties at home and at work, someone who would grow up to be like a sister, a best friend, a girl in the image of her own mother.

Saba thought of the moment she told her mother of her own dream, that she wanted to be a doctor, not a domestic servant. And Saba flew on her chosen path. One of the best students we have ever taught, her head teacher remarked. Every year Saba was alone when she received another award for excellence. Without her mother or brother, she sat with her favourite teacher, an Ethiopian woman who taught science, to draw up a study plan that would have taken her all the way to a university in the capital city. She had to orphan herself to reach her goals.

Saba's eyes returned to her mother. Their battles against each other had created an unbridgeable distance. And Saba wondered if they could ever love each other again. Hagos would know how. He cooked for their mother, washed and ironed her clothes, massaged her when her back was aching, and made her ginger juice to soothe her heartburn.

I will make up for it when I finish my studies, Saba had vowed back then. Catching up on the lost love after graduation, as Doctor Saba.

The fragrance of frying onions and garlic rose in the air but was soon overpowered as the breeze carried the stench of the open toilet again into the square. Saba and Hagos sat on a blanket outside their hut.

Hagos stretched his legs on the ground, resting his head on Saba's lap. He smelt of butter. Since they had run out of medication for his recurrent headaches, the midwife had advised their mother to massage his head with ghee every night before bedtime. The jar borrowed from Samhiya's mother was half empty.

Saba stroked her brother's temples, massaged the thick ropes of his veins. The collar of her white chemise fluttered in the breeze. This nightgown of her older cousin was loose on her. Before Saba left her hometown, her cousin gave Saba some of the wedding clothes bought by her husband as a gift. Everyone knew, though, it was Hagos who'd helped their cousin's husband to choose these wedding presents. Silent men are the best readers of a woman, the cousin used to say.

Hagos's eyes were shut. Her thighs cooked under his ghee-soaked head on this warm evening. But Saba didn't push him away. The priest and the imam of their hometown had been in rare agreement when their mother asked them for a divine cure for her son's muteness. She should instead celebrate what God has given him, they said. His innocence, his guilelessness, a good heart, and thus a guaranteed place in heaven.

Hagos had chosen Saba's black dress too. When she wore it for the first time, the mother grabbed the dress by its collar. It showed too much of Saba's legs, the mother said. It was too tight around her hips.

I am not returning it, said Saba. The mother slapped her that day. But Saba took her mother's wrath without revealing the dress was Hagos's choice. This was more than a dress. He had chosen something that fitted her like the skin she had lost.

Saba was used to bearing things on his behalf, even knowing that by doing so she helped maintain his perfection in her mother's eyes, and in everyone else's. When Hagos came home drunk one night and the mother smelt alcohol in the courtyard the following morning, Saba stepped forward and begged forgiveness. The mother forbade Saba from venturing out in the evenings and hit her palms with a stick. Saba had not been able to do her homework for days. But Hagos, Saba was certain, loved her too, even though she had taken his place at school. He taught her how to swim in the wild river, away from people and away from the unwritten rule that girls shouldn't swim. He made sure Saba would never drown like some girls in their hometown. He washed and ironed her school uniform, drawing out the creases even from the inside pockets, made her egg sandwiches, sharpened her pencils.

Eventually, Hagos stood up and went inside the hut. In one corner of the square, young men played football. The athlete rose high to head a red sock ball flicked by his co-striker into an imaginary net. Not far from the football match, a few men were talking, too far away for her to eavesdrop, but the seriousness that accompanied their gesticulations made Saba think they were discussing politics. Agonizing over the independence fight, perhaps, about how rebels in shorts and rubber sandals, armed with Kalashnikovs, were going to defeat an enemy equipped with tanks and fighter planes. The men shouted. Freedom. Freedom. Freedom.

Samhiya was giggling to the whispers of the athlete who had abandoned the football game to play with her manicured fingers. Ahead of the happy pair, children carried each other piggyback. From the dust swirling in the air, a young man emerged wearing a waistcoat over his long robe, jumping up and down in front of his family, his feet beating on the foreign soil, the edge of his sword sparkling in his stretched arm, brandishing the weapon of gallantry to defeat the pain of exile.

The football match resumed. The barefoot athlete manipulated the ball with his toes and exchanged passes with his co-striker before scooping it above Samhiya, who ignored the game and strutted with swaying hips straight through the ranks of watching children.

When the ball landed on the roof of a hut, the athlete hauled a boy against its wall. The boy shook the thatch until the red sock ball rolled from the yellow roof.

Hagos returned to the blanket with Saba's black dress. She had ripped the side as she collected firewood in the bush earlier that day with Zahra and Samhiya. Her mother said that Saba had brought her clumsiness with her when they fled their home. The idea that habits flee with people wherever they go terrified Saba. There was no new beginning anywhere, she thought. The same people in a different place. Memories from home shuffled through her head, her room, her bed, her teacher, her best friend, the doum palm tree, books, rain, the Mareb river, a plan to take her to Addis University, dergue soldiers, death, dreams in the field of sorghum, her bed, her naked body at dawn.

Saba turned towards the brightest side of the square. The flame of an oil lamp flickered against Hagos's face, drawing out the concentration in his eyes as he sewed the rip in the dress.

One thing Saba had left back home was her talkativeness. People used to say she talked for both of them. Not any more. Her silence, though, was temporary. Just like her brother's. When she was little, she always believed that Hagos would talk one day, and often fixed her eyes on his mouth, waiting to be the first to hear him utter his first word.

There was a scar in the corner of his lower lip. So subtle was this cut that it appeared designed to ease the load of the unsaid words. God is merciful this way, she thought, standing now.

Saba told Hagos that she needed to go to the open field. He put the dress aside and looked up at her, his mouth half open. A long time ago, he used to try to force himself to talk, to force out words. But every time he did, it was as though each word was a large, sharp object carving the back of his throat. His cheeks inflated. His eyes widened and tears welled up in his eyes. Only incomprehensible sounds left his lips. He had stopped trying.

Hagos signalled to Saba to wait. Dusk settled on the thatched roofs. Darkness like thick ink splotched on the walls, and between the alleys, wood-burning stoves glowed red from the black ground.

Hagos took a torch and beckoned her forward.

I'll be fine going alone, Saba said.

In his company, she was economical with words. Hagos walked forward. His inability to argue made him decisive in her mind.

On catching up, she held his hand. Hagos turned to the right of the hut. Saba assumed he took this route, even though the fastest way to the toilet was straight ahead from the hut and through the east of the camp, to avoid the crowd in the square. Hagos jumped over a shrub and flicked aside an empty sardine can that rolled towards Saba. A scorpion latched onto her sandal. She shook it off her foot. The scorpion darted across the lane.

The wind pushed a door to her right open. Saba saw a man defecating in a pot, a woman caressing his head. His cries for a doctor faded as she sped up behind her brother. Privacy was mixed with the dung and sand when this camp was constructed, Saba thought. She had figured out by now that the huts were built in no order and without proper planning. They were scattered around, with some having more space between them than others. Some of the lanes were so narrow that only two people at most could pass at a time. And doors faced each other. Refugees, Saba thought, were all the same, the same as each other, the same as the shrubs, the same as the hibiscus, the same as shit and piss, the same as the sky and earth.

Some had brought their beds outside to sleep in the open air. Hagos dimmed his torch as they negotiated their way between hands and feet dangling from beds. When Saba tried to avoid a young man sitting at the feet of a woman braiding his hair, she almost stepped on the white shells laid out by a fortune teller. Hagos steadied his sister, but as she moved aside to let the midwife and the judge through, Saba pushed against a door to her left. Through the slit, she noticed a woman bending low to blow on the charcoals of an open furnace. Her skirt lifted and crawled up on her skin.

Saba looked away but noticed Hagos's eyes lingering on the woman, who had managed to ignite the charcoals, the fire of the furnace rising and flickering between her dark thighs.

Saba could not stop thinking about what had just happened as they arrived at the open toilet. Hagos's manhood hadn't been extinguished because he was disabled, like her cousin and her friends back home had assumed. Saba turned to Hagos and embraced him, letting go of his warm body when it occurred to her she might be interrupting a beautiful moment in his head.

They arrived at the last rows of huts yet to be occupied. New refugees are on the way, the English aid coordinator explained to Saba when she had asked if she could move with her family into this quarter. The open field, which the refugees shared as a toilet, didn't disturb her any longer, it was the crowd in the square, the noise, the endless talking, the screams, it was living life under the nose of everyone else that she couldn't get used to. Hagos raised his torch. The long grass parted and three girls emerged out of the darkness. The girls mumbled their greetings as they strode past brother and sister.

Hagos bent to the ground and looked around, picking up smooth stones for Saba to wipe herself with after she had finished. Saba walked into the field. Grass caressed her arms. An insect bit her. Mosquito? Or a fat beetle depositing shit in her skin? She was about to sit when she heard loud, repeated coughs. Saba advanced forward until she found a quiet spot. She searched for other dangers. The afternoon before, a woman had encountered a viper and men armed with sticks came to clear the area. But there were still many snakes about.

She shone the torch here over there here again over there again. A grasshopper landed on the grass in front of her. The leaf quivered when something slithered in the grass, Saba leapt to her feet and wet her underwear as she scampered away.

THE MIDWIFE

The confrontation began when a man arrived in the square holding a bag of miswak sticks and declared his price for each teeth-cleaning twig.

Can't you see people are standing in front of the aid centre? a mother with a child said.

This is business, the man said. I am not a charity.

Don't be callous, said a woman to the seller. I saw you climbing the peelu tree deep in the bush.

Men surrounded the miswak seller, telling him the twigs belonged to everyone in the camp.

A man snatched the seller's bag. The struggle ensued. The judge arrived. A trial was called at the judge's hut.

Saba didn't attend the trial but the verdict reached her: No one owns anything in the camp, the judge had said after listening to the seller and residents of the camp. We all share everything.

We share everything, Saba repeated to herself as she sat next to Hagos while he lit the three-stone stove over the ground. He placed a pot with water on the fire. Saba saw the bag full of flour by his foot. He opened a jar of tesmi. It was empty. Hagos furrowed his eyebrows. Saba understood he was making ga'at porridge but that he didn't have ghee. Telling Hagos to wait, Saba took a bag of lentils from their jute sack and ran to Zahra's hut, returning soon with the ghee she had swapped for the lentils.

Four girls carrying buckets stood nearby on their way home from the river. They laughed as Hagos stirred flour into the boiling water to make the porridge. Curse on you, one of the girls said to Saba. Why are you making him cook?

Saba waved them off with her hand. The girls walked away, now and then turning their heads back to stare at Saba. Hagos, unperturbed, scooped some of the porridge onto a plate, adding ghee and chilli.

Saba watched as a queue formed outside the aid centre. Aid workers with long sticks kept order. Here, adults were disciplined too. An eagle flew over the camp and landed on the thatched roof of the aid centre. An old man waiting in the queue aimed his stick at it. We have nothing. Go away. Go.

Saba gasped as the large bird sailed over the old man's head, its claws gliding past his white turban, and snatched a piece of sardine from a young girl feeding her younger brother.

As Saba joined the queue, she noticed men with naked wrists. Watches probably broken, she thought, or batteries dead or saved for a place where time mattered, when one often heard I don't have the time or I will be there pronto or what time do you call this? Batteries saved for when there was an office to go to, a school to attend, a doctor to visit, a garage to open, a police station to manage. Saba wondered how something you had in abundance, relative to others, lost meaning. Time faded into insignificance.

An anguished scream shot through all other noises in the square. Laughter ceased. Babies hushed. Arguments postponed. Where is the midwife? My son is dying, called a man, stumbling across the camp and carrying a boy who had vomit down his shirt.

The children who were playing hide-and-seek deserted the game. Their shadows disentangled behind them as they ran off in different directions to search for the midwife. From her place in the queue, Saba's eyes roamed the square. The midwife was nowhere to be seen. The camp had no medical centre and so the midwife, who specialized in herbal medicine and basic nursing alongside her usual duties as a midwife, was in constant demand. As she brought life into this world, she was now tasked with sustaining it.

The midwife was the only woman consulted by the committee of elders, and she no longer had to cook, wash or clean. Every patient she treated vowed to her a lifetime of servitude.

I saw her at my neighbour's hut, his child is ill too, said a man, pointing to the south of the camp, as he joined the queue next to Saba.

No, she is in the north attending a pregnant woman, said another.

But the midwife was already running barefoot towards the sick child. Saba spotted herbal medicine tied in one part of her scarf, and the sand coiling in the air behind her made it seem as if she was transformed into a storm. Saba shut her eyes.

The light-skinned midwife was born to two of the darkest people in their border town. God has forgiven all our sins, her tearful parents declared at her arrival, setting their fair-skinned daughter on a path of strict upbringing. Saba was captivated by the midwife's green eyes, lush even at times of drought, and by the mole under her nose, the only dark spot on her body that linked her to her parents. But what most astonished young Saba was that the midwife always smelled of fresh incense. She later discovered that the midwife tied frankincense gum in her scarf which she chewed throughout the day and that every evening she draped a thick sheet over herself to bathe in the sandalwood fumes of an incense burner. As well as making her skin glow, the incense made her sweat, increasing her appetite. Her husband had loved her voluptuousness.

The boy didn't die.

But death came soon after, dressed in yellow.

On the morning of the colourful funeral, Saba and Zahra arrived at Samhiya's hut to take her with them to fetch wood. Samhiya was filing her nails. Sit on the bed, ladies, this will take me some time, said Samhiya. I still need to paint my nails.

Why? asked Zahra. We are just going to fetch wood.

A city girl has her secrets, Samhiya said, laughing.

Saba gaped around the room and felt as if she had stepped back in time. Samhiya's hut had two beds, a big mirror, make-up, a wardrobe, shoes, chickpeas, onions, potatoes, shoro, kitchen equipment, knives, a chopping board, cups, plates, coffee-making materials. They too had escaped the war, yet they managed to bring all this.

The more she looked into other people's huts, the more Saba noticed differences in mindset. Some fled with mattresses and pillows, others with coffee machines or cooking utensils or clothes. And Saba suspected it might not have been the lack of money to pay the smuggler for extra possessions that prevented her mother from fleeing with more, but rather that their mother had left valuable belongings so that they would always think of returning home. Memories alone were not enough to tie someone to a land, they faded with distance and the passage of time.

But Saba wondered too if her mother had worried that some of the neighbours staying behind would talk and place a curse on the family if they were to see her taking not only her children but also her belongings, while they couldn't afford to take themselves out of the war zone.

Finally, the girls arrived at the forest. The bush was less threatening, it had lost some of its density, the vastness that had made it seem so impregnable in the beginning. Without charcoal, the camp's residents relied on the bush's wood for fuel.

The grass underneath Saba's feet shifted in the wind. She rubbed her scalp with her index finger so she wouldn't loosen the bandana that Hagos had rolled and wrapped around her head, pulling her thick hair up into a tight bun. Ahead of her, Samhiya, in a floral dress that hugged her curves, observed a flower emerging from the cracks between the rocks.

The breeze brought the aroma of the city from Samhiya's perfumed neck to Saba. Saba inhaled, as if Samhiya's fragrance was something she could carry to Hagos like she carried the water on her head, the firewood on her back. Saba smiled at the thought.

When they had collected as much wood as they could carry, they helped each other tie bundles on their backs using their scarves.

Zahra stooped over the green field and picked wild spinach leaves for her grandmother.

As Saba bent next to Zahra, the bundle of wood on her back rolled to her nape, cutting into her skin.

Vafanculo.

Language, ladies, said Samhiya.

Only a well-maintained lady like you minds her language, said Saba, pressing leaves on the fresh wound.

I think someone is jealous, said Samhiya. I shouldn't have shown off my snake skin.

The girls burst out laughing.

Saba gave some of the bundle of wild leaves she had collected to Zahra.

Saba, are you all right?

Yes.

Silence.

Saba, you talk less and less. It must be hard living with Hagos.

Hagos is not mute to me, said Saba. Maybe if you ever listened to him you would hear him too.

I'm sorry, Zahra said.

Hagos is not mute. But the world is not prepared to listen.

Saba swayed as she pushed herself up. Zahra held her arm. They rose together. I will learn to listen to him then, Zahra said as she applied more leaves to the wound at Saba's nape. The blood stopped.

I could smell rain in the air, Samhiya said.

The trees around them shuddered. The incipient whistle of the forest brought music that echoed in the valley.

As they trudged back home Zahra told the story of the day her mother had left for the trenches. I was eight, she said. It was early morning, my mother and I hadn't slept all night long. My mother sat against the bed and I rested my head on her chest and cried. When the morning came, I had never hated the sun as much as that day. I hoped it would disappear, that our life would be one long night.

The three girls resumed walking in silence, their young backs arching under the heavy bundles. A raindrop landed on Saba's forehead. The wind blew harder. They hurried on the pathway that was now obscured by whirling sand.

And then the rain poured down.

Let's take cover under the tree, Saba said.

They joined hands to support each other against the wind and rain, their shoulders pushing against the invisible wall. The firewood squeaked against their backs. Once in the shelter of the eucalyptus tree, they stood panting. Saba looked in the distance where the rain had cleared the red sand off large rocks.

Samhiya took off her wet dress and hung it over the nearest branch. Can you wipe my back, bella? she asked, passing her scarf to Saba.

Saba gaped at the curvy body in matching bra and pants. She chased the drops of rain on the flesh that clung to Samhiya's hips. Saba thought of Hagos, and hooked her fingers into the side of Samhiya's underwear. Samhiya twitched.

These are the handles for a man to carry me to bed with, Samhiya said, laughing.

As if that man was Hagos and Hagos was her, Saba firmed her grip on Samhiya's sides.

Ouch, Saba, stop it, said Samhiya. It hurts.

Saba let go. Hagos, like a brief sensation, fleeted away from her thoughts. Her heart quietened. She shuffled to adjust the weight of the bundle she carried. Samhiya's oiled back glistened in the sunlight breaking through the clouds. Saba touched Samhiya's silver necklace. Where did you get this? she asked.

I can lend it to you, but only if you get married before me, Samhiya responded.

You can keep your fancy necklace. I am not going to marry before I finish school.

School? In this camp? Please tell us this is a joke, Saba.

I asked the English aid worker and he told me school was coming soon, Saba said. They have already allocated the field in the south of the camp.

Aid workers promise anything to get rid of people, Saba. Do you know how many people queue to ask questions and request this and that? You could build a palace in the air out of their promises.

Saba swerved around Samhiya and pushed through the rain.

By the time they had returned to the camp, the sky was clear and the soil had dried out in the blazing sun. As they entered the square they went their separate ways. Close to her hut, Saba noticed a woman dressed in a long yellow gown standing in the square, the woman whose jerrycan Hagos had saved from the river. Saba waved. The woman closed her eyes and started singing an aria in both Italian and Tigrinya, her voice rising as if to silence the waning thunder. Saba dropped the firewood by her hut. She was drenched in sweat. Her dress, having lost a few buttons and its lustre a while back, stuck to her skin. A few threads pulled away from the bottom of the dress. Her body felt as torn.

The woman hugged herself, digging her long yellow nails into her skin. She shook, fell to her knees and collapsed.

Saba ran to find the midwife, bringing her back to a crowd that had gathered outside their hut, where Hagos had carried the woman. The midwife entered but exited moments later. Our daughter left us, she said. God bless her soul.

There was a long silence.

She's dead, the midwife said.

The elders bowed their heads. Saba wondered if death in this place that was supposed to be safe caught them by surprise too. She had bought the illusion that escaping the war meant escaping all forms of death. Otherwise, why go through the pain of exile to come here?

Many women wept, mourning the passing of a beautiful woman who arrived at the camp wearing the colour of the sun. When the athlete came with a shovel borrowed from the aid centre, the elders didn't move. They had yet to decide on a burial site. The athlete said he knew a large swathe of flat land, south of the camp. We need to cut the grass and it will be ready, he said.

No, not that place, it is where they will build the school, Saba said, shouting above the wailing mourners. It is not for a graveyard. It is for our future.

The midwife pulled Saba by the hand and shoved her inside the hut where the dead woman was laid out on her blanket.

The morning after a rainy night. The morning after the death. Rays of sunshine fell on the camp. On Saba's face. The crowded square. A man lathered the face of another with a soaped brush in front of a broken mirror hanging from the wall. Saba was blind to her fragmented reflection in the mirror, but noticed a half-white, half-black face, head tilting to the side. A razor pressed against the cheek. A trickle of blood. A woman hung dresses, trousers, shirts, a jellabiya and vests on the clothesline as a girl ground grain into flour on a stone. Cries. Laughter. Moaning. And mourning. The fragrance of incense drifted from another hut. A girl's toes polished in red stuck out of the dung-fed mud wall. When Saba turned, the imam and the priest bumped into each other in a lane where only one could pass. Both men raised their hands in supplication. Saba walked on. A scream. A woman having sex. Hagos stormed her mind as she peeked through the window as the man's thing drowned inside the woman. A woman's inside is made of sea, Saba thought. Seaweed. Fish. Balloons. Bags. Love letters in bottles floating endlessly. Sadness. Laughter. This woman's inside contains her womb, the seeds of a future and now his dick. How deep was a woman? Saba asked herself. A man wept: I found God, his tears fall on the holy book. I too, a woman. Me too, a girl. We too. We too. A family. God proliferating in a place abandoned by humanity. Chants. Igziabeher. Allah. God. Rebbee. Credo in Dio. Ululations. Elelelelelel. Too much to take. Too much. Saba held her head in her hands. Dizziness. Vomit gushed out of her. She closed her eyes. She fainted.

Where is the midwife?

Has anyone seen the midwife?

It was Hagos stirring in his sleep who revived her.

THE TELEVISION

Saba was on her way back home from visiting the grave of the dead opera singer in the new graveyard, which was situated in a field north of the camp between the river and the open field, when she noticed Jamal sitting out and working by an oil lamp on a big cardboard box outside his hut. A cigarette dangled from the corner of his lips. The ex-cinema worker had announced the day before, as he marched away from the aid centre with two empty boxes, that television was coming to the camp. Delusional, said a few of those waiting for their food under the scorching sun. Delusional, others repeated. Labels and nicknames proliferated in this place of scarcity, as if they added to self-worth.

Not far from Jamal, two old men in colourful cardigans were talking about Asmara. Saba edged closer.

As far as I can remember, said a bald, clean-shaven man wearing a pink jumper, Cahsai sold his jewellery shop when the British defeated the fascists in Keren's mountains. He had heard that once the British colonized a nation, they ransacked all its wealth. So, in a village only accessible by donkey, he hid his valuables under his mother's pillow.

It's too long ago, said his white-haired companion, who wore a blue cardigan with a gabi wrapped around his legs. You are too old for these detailed memories. Funny, though, how you seem to remember the bad things about the British while forgetting our life under Italian fascism.

I disagree, said the bald man, throwing his hand in air that was saturated with Jamal's smoke. With age, we become selective, not forgetful. I recall a few things and I choose to remember the stories of love and passion. Cahsai's wife, Madam Hadith, for example. I was having coffee on her veranda when she told me that Cahsai was going to the capital for business. She had a sad glint in her eyes then. She knew her husband had a lover in that city. A woman from the conquerors' land took his heart, she cried. I held her. But how do you console a person dispossessed from love and land? Her shivering body that day awoke the heart I thought I lost when I saw what the Italians did to my father, God bless his soul.

But what has this story got to do with Italian fascism? said the white-haired man, as Jamal's smoke circled above his head. This proves my point. You are old and mixing up stories. Like our land, our minds and memories have been franchised between the different European countries. That's our tragedy.

The bald man shook his head. Ascolta, mia cara, he said to Saba in Italian. Saba sat down and leaned against the hut. She turned to her right. Jamal was drawing Benito Mussolini on a piece of cardboard that he had pegged on a clothesline between two huts in this lane. Saba's attention returned to the bald man, who pulled his handkerchief from his cardigan pocket and rubbed his watering eyes. He continued his story: Madam Hadith, though, understood. That love can come from unexpected places and in its tide one can drift. We kissed. I was fifteen, and she was about to enter her fifties.

Saba was sitting next to Hagos on their blanket outside the hut when Jamal ambled past them. Television is here, announced some of the children marching behind him. We don't need electricity to watch television.

Hagos, let's go and watch, Saba said, about to stand up.

Hagos held her by her wrist. He gestured.

Why do I need to wait?

Hagos disappeared inside the hut and returned with a bag. He sat behind her on a stool. Saba looked at the giggling girls and boys gathered in front of them. The TV is over there, she said. Hagos pulled her head towards him. Rubbing her hair with almond oil, he straightened it with the bristle brush. Saba wondered if he had a crush on the Indian actress they once saw in a magazine back home. His obsession with changing her curly hair began then, as far as she could recall. He pinned a flower on the side of her hair. After spraying her neck with some of his perfume, he rose and pulled her up.

Saba and Hagos arrived at a dimmed part of the square where Jamal placed the cardboard box, his television, on a stool, next to an oil lamp shining from an adjacent stool.

The children jumped up and down, urging Jamal to hurry up.

Saba sat next to Hagos in the front row. Mosquitoes buzzed in and out of the open TV box. The little actors emerged in the soft glow of the lamp.

They are here, the children said. The actors are here. Let's wave.

The applause and the whistles attracted more spectators. Zahra arrived with her grandmother, who was holding a wooden mortar and pestle full of roasted coffee beans. The old woman declined a stool and instead squatted on the ground, beginning to grind the beans. I will stop when the television starts, she assured the children. The black powder scattered in the wind. Samhiya's mother appeared too, saying she had caught a whiff of the grandmother's Harar coffee.

Here, take it, I will come to drink coffee at yours after the show, said the grandmother, handing to Samhiya's mother the coffee she had ground in the mortar.

Jamal slipped his cardboard characters, an Italian mother and her young daughter made from white cardboard, into the TV from a hole at the top. The women stood in front of the image of Mussolini drawn at the back of the box.

The Italian women were silent as if they were suffering from stage fright. When Jamal coughed, the cardboard puppets shook.

Saba waved at the Italian girl who, as narrated by Jamal, was in the luxurious living room of a villa in Tiravolo, Asmara's posh residential neighbourhood.

The girl staggered to her mother on the other side of the soggiorno, pleading with her to understand that she was in love with a local man.

Saba leaned her head on Hagos's shoulder as Jamal went on to tell this story of impossible love.

The mother turned her head away from Signorina. When a European country colonizes an African land, there is always this risk, she said. Our leaders have, in anticipation of such a thing, calculated for unfortunate situations like yours, just like taking into account African diseases.

SIGNORINA: My love is not a disease, Mother. And how about my father's affairs with una nera?

MADRE: You know how men are, darling. They like to conquer a land and its people. The onus is on us to keep the purity of our race. This weight on a woman's shoulders is a blessing from God.

SIGNORINA: Well, I am accountable to no one, Mother. I love him. I don't care that he is an African.

MADRE: Love is a package. Other things are as important.

SIGNORINA: I was born here. I am African too.

MADRE: Hahahaha. Your naivety, daughter, knows no limit.

Your stupidity knows no limit, said a boy in the audience, quickly hushed by others.

SIGNORINA: He is different.

MADRE: You are right. He is different. He wears different clothes to his people. He wants to please you so much that he lost his roots.

SIGNORINA: It is not a weakness to be intrigued, to love something different from you. If he is weak so am I.

MADRE: I am tired of this. I will not tolerate a young girl questioning me.

SIGNORINA: I know, Mother. My sweetheart is rejected by his side and by ours. But his roots are in my heart, as mine are in his.

Wild applause.
Shush. Shush.

PADRE (a large frame puppet, waking from his siesta in the veranda,
yelling at Signorina): Never shout at your mother. Now go out
and don't come back until you have reflected upon what you
have said.
Signorina weeps.

A few children stood up and screamed at the father. You shut up,
fattening yourself with the wealth of our land. A boy kicked dust at the
TV. The Italian family turned brown. A chorus of nationalistic song
erupted. Freedom. Freedom.

The call to freedom drew the singer. She played her krar, which started
a dance around the TV that only stopped when Zahra's grandmother
called for calm. Turning to the TV, the old woman addressed the Italian
father. He had regained his white skin after Jamal blew the dust off his
face. The grandmother wagged her finger at the father, scolding him in
his own language for his treatment of his daughter. She then reached
with her hand through the hole in the box and stroked Signorina's face.
All women, black and white, are going through hard times, she said
to the girl: Ma come, mia figlia, so che combatti per i tuoi diritti. Non
dovresti mollare mai.

Zahra applauded. Standing up, she told the children around her: Yes,
she will not give up. Like my mother, she will fight for her rights.

Jamal placed a coloured picture of Cinema Impero, where he had
worked, at the back of the box. I know this cinema, said the Khwaja.
Bella Asmara, he sang. Bella Asmara. Piccola Roma of Africa. Where
stars are reachable from your turf because you are the high and mighty
of all cities.

Quiet, please.

Saba waved at the Khwaja. The Khwaja nodded: Buonasera.

Jamal slipped in a brown puppet. Signorina Patricia was watching a
film at Cinema Impero in Mussolini Avenue. Dawit, forbidden access
to the whites-only cinema, waited for the signorina outside behind a

palm tree, his black skin helping him to remain invisible. Smoke that Jamal blew through a hole in the boy's head coiled in front of Dawit. Saba squinted and followed Dawit through the fog of Asmara's high mountains as she paced up and down. As the signorina exited, Dawit ran to her and they embraced on the footpath. Behind them chatters of disgust grew. Jamal leaned over the TV and blew his breath through the hole. Asmara's winter wind bit the signorina. The Italian girl shivered in her lover's arms.

The lovers retreated to the back street.

Another round of applause. And loud cheers: Yes. Yes.

As if emboldened, Dawit's voice grew: Let's go to my house.

In a bed made of a sardine tin and covered in thatch, a sheet of paper for pillows, the signorina and Dawit lay down.

SIGNORINA: Do you hate my parents?

DAWIT: Patricia, we are not original. Our story is a repetition. And the end is known to both of us.

SIGNORINA: Yet we choose to engage in a story with a foregone conclusion.

DAWIT: We are humans. We like a good fight because we think we can win where others have failed.

Dawit and Patricia embrace each other.

Padre breaks down the door. Gun in hand.

The first show of the camp television had long ended. People had retreated into their huts. Hagos was asleep. Saba closed the door and stood outside. She noticed Jamal in the distance, surrounded by the committee of the elders. The midwife arrived with the athlete, who had rolled up his sleeves. His yelling overlaid the chorus of crickets rising from the bush. The air cooled down.

Mosquitoes buzzed around her, their thirst for her blood seeming to have intensified with the arrival of the moon. Squatting down on the ground, Saba unwrapped the scarf from her neck and spread it over her shoulders, covering the flesh that appeared through holes of her dress, on her back, on the side of her arms. Saba contemplated the new mosquito bites on her forearm and felt the bump on her forehead from when she had walked into the pole of the hut earlier. A swelling on her foot had appeared, a scorpion sting. Her skin swelled in parts and Saba imagined herself rising up like a balloon. Rising above the shrub, above the men fighting Jamal, above the camp and gliding towards the starred sky.

She heard Jamal yell. The athlete snatched the puppets out of the ex-cinema worker's hands. He ripped up the cardboard characters and flung the pieces into the air. Jamal flitted past Saba like a shadow. Behind him, the lovers' carved-up bodies scattered on the moonlit ground. The lovers died twice that night, Saba pondered, thinking back to that last scene when Dawit and Signorina had made love under the threat of death.

Saba made her way back to the hut. The oil lamp flickered, the flame dancing across Hagos's face. Saba stepped over him and sat on her side of the blanket.

The blanket had aged. Hagos had patched up some of the holes by sewing colourful fabric onto the grey blanket. Green. Pink. Red. Yellow, the colour of the deceased woman's dress. Every time she sat on the blanket, Saba felt the spirit of the woman as if her corpse had remained on the same blanket. Saba pressed against the jagged surface of the curved wall. The dazzling yellow dress sparkled to the stars shining through the window. The deceased threw her arms around Hagos and hugged him tighter. Death became animated on his warm body. Yellow paint melted on his skin. On a rivulet of his sweat a yellow hibiscus flower flourished.

No matter how often Saba washed the blanket and scrubbed it by the river, the memory of death appeared woven into the fabric. That night, though, as she closed her eyes, it was the bodies of Dawit and Signorina that stayed at the forefront of her mind. She wondered if the smile on Hagos's sleeping face was ignited by that same scene. Saba blew out the lamp.

The next morning, Saba felt the sun burn as it filtered through the window. Warm air pressed against her chest. Beads of sweat trickled down her body as she rocked from side to side. Saba could smell her own skin, muddy and damp. Her mind was drawn back to when she was young, unburdened by guilt, or by society's expectations of her. The world wasn't confrontational then, because Saba hadn't yet conjured up a dream. In those days, she and her mother talked and laughed. In those days, her thighs, like the rest of her body, were unscarred.

Saba opened her eyes and sat up, breathless. She was naked, her chemise lying at the end of her feet, near Hagos's head. She stared at her own bare legs, at the scars of healed wounds. Hagos had his hand around her shin. He placed his black foot on her purple thigh.

Saba dressed and exited the hut and stood by the door staring into the empty square. She slid against the outside wall, next to the remains of the orange seedlings, which had died a long time ago. Only repulsion could grow in this place.

She wrapped her arms around herself. It wasn't Hagos's fault. Most of her male relatives, younger than he, were already married, had children. In comparison, Hagos had sympathy. Sweet Hagos. That was what her cousin and her friends called him. Shukor, innocent Hagos.

Saba stood up and peered through the window. Hagos hugged her nightwear in his arms as if a woman lay next to him.

The square was deserted. Saba breathed in the air that was hers alone. Before long, people began to stream onto the square. It dawned on Saba that there were no animals in this place. She longed for dogs. To stroke cats. Drink fresh milk. Have eggs. She longed to eat chicken stew, fried goat with berbere and lentils. The dust made her cough.

It was a ration day. Queuing offered a purpose of some sort for Saba. In the absence of an aim to work towards, the aid centre became a focal point. Like going to the forest for wood, to the river for water.

Saba joined the queue with those whose coupons specified Saturday. To her right, a few men sat in a circle playing cards. They would be playing all day long. Samhiya and her mother waved at Saba. They were chatting as they walked to the river. The sun glistened on the metal buckets they balanced on their heads. The heat seeped into her skin and Saba sweltered in her black dress. The English aid coordinator rolled up his sleeves and unbuttoned his shirt. He seemed to take energy from the same sun that sucked her dry.

Saba queued instead of her brother. If he could talk, she was sure, he would have done it. If silence was a language, she would not have forced herself to be his voice. She talked to people even when she didn't feel like it. She queued for hours to ask the aid centre questions about better food, better clothes, for her, her mother and Hagos. She bore the scorching sun as she waited for food, and like the trips to the river to fetch water or wash clothes, or to the bush to collect firewood, it marked its presence on her body.

By contrast, Hagos's skin was smooth. Even after one of his journeys into the wild, nature would not leave a trace on his body. There were no marks of thorns on his legs, no cactus milk on his arms. He glided through the bush as he did among people, unnoticed, unmarked.

Saba had given all her femininity to her brother. She remembered the midwife's words about Hagos. But Saba didn't have enough femininity to give, just as Hagos didn't have enough masculinity to give her. They were born like that. But what struck Saba the more she thought about the statement that the midwife made, and that others had made about her and Hagos, was how they saw household chores as what defined being a woman. It was more than chores. Hagos allowed the woman in him to direct his life, the way he felt, the way he moved through life. Saba saw it in his freedom, his boldness to be himself, his ability to be gentle and strong. He made his presence felt not by shouting himself to the front, but by holding himself together despite all his wounds, to shine even in the dark.

Saba's thoughts were interrupted when the man behind her in the queue pushed, his weight pinning her against the man in front. Squeezed, Saba couldn't move. When she felt a state of passivity between the two men, she squirmed herself out of the queue and wandered off without direction. When she arrived in the south of the camp, she realized she was on the road that connected the camp with the rest of this country, the road used by the workers that led to somewhere, a village, a town, another country, a river or a cliff or the sea. A road, nevertheless, Saba mumbled to herself. A road that led to freedom.

Refugees are easy to police, the Khwaja once said. The authorities know that fear and ignorance of our surroundings makes it cheaper and easier to keep us here. But one day, one of us will break this fear and ignorance and be free. When he said this, the Khwaja punched his fist in the air, as if breaking through invisible walls.

But was it freedom she was looking for? Saba could have been happy in the camp if there had been a school. Freedom, Saba realized now, meant different things to different people. The Khwaja wanted to read his newspaper, as he told her once, on the day of publication. With a cup of espresso, as I used to do in Asmara, he said, his voice rising to a high pitch.

Zahra wanted to help her mother with her quest to free a country, while Hagos didn't need an independent country or a school or a job. He was as carefree in the camp as he was back home.

Saba looked around her. There was nothing. Not even evidence that the aid coordinator's Land Rover had driven through here earlier in the morning, the marks of his car's wheels on the sandy road wiped out. Which way was the way out? Saba wondered. She fixed her eyes on the dusty empty road ahead. Through this desiccated umbilical cord came the Englishman and his staff, came the lorries with sardines, oil and sugar. She stood on her toes, as if by doing so she would be able to see the rest of this country on the horizon. The country their lorry driver had sung about on their journey to the camp.

As Saba walked she imagined a lush village by the bend of the Nile. Tractors working the fields, hot loaves of bread sold from the back of bicycles, women in thobes standing in front of blackboards with chalk in their hands, students in school uniform hurrying through passageways full of life.

Saba's legs felt light. She sprinted. The few trees populating the road at the beginning of the camp were behind her now. She tripped and fell on her knees, breathless and thirsty. This was not the way to freedom but to loss.

On her way back to the camp, Saba stopped by the large field at the south designated by the aid workers as the place for the future school. Unlike the open toilet, this field was left untouched. Nature lived freely here and grass grew stubbornly in this dry place, it expanded into the horizon and reached the height of her ribcage. Saba wondered how long it would take for a school to be built in this spot of land.

Things would have been different, she thought, if the authorities had built the camp near the city. Nearer to a school or a college or university. She remembered the moment on their journey to the camp when she thought that was the case, when their lorry had left the outskirts of the city which they had arrived at on camels, and Saba had seen tents on the side of the asphalt highway. Is this the refugee camp? she asked the driver.

No, said Tahir. They are nomads, he said, pointing to the men in jellabiyas and the women in black veils. Saba slumped back into the seat as the Rashaida's tents flicked by, the city fading in the side mirror, the fragrance of ripe mangoes and ripe bananas waning. The road in the middle of the desert, its black tarmac shimmering under the sun. Express buses were overtaking the lorry. Each carried a promise of rapid arrival to the capital painted onto its sides. Their advertisements were meant for free people. Saba already felt trapped inside a moving prison.

A lizard raised its head and stared at Saba. A gatekeeper in graceful pose. Saba walked into the field, towards the rock she often sat on. With each foot pressing, the blades of grass leaned forward. A ladybird flew and landed on her hand. Saba wanted to make a wish when the bug flew off. She stretched her arm in a vain attempt to catch it.

Once deeper into the field, she sat on her rock – wheezing and out of breath – where she closed her eyes, imagining herself in the future, in a classroom in a school built in this field, surrounded by the smell of books and ink. Saba hugged her knees and rocked back and forth as she looked out over the plumes of grass that lapped against each other in the wind. Something rustled in the grass next to her. A girl's manicured hands appeared through the thick grass. Saba jerked back on her rock. Her eyes followed the long fingernails digging into the dry ground.

Saba retreated to the other side of the rock, hiding behind a cactus plant. The girl moaned.

Stop, Saba heard a girl's voice say, sounding as familiar as the other one who asked: Why?

Well, my love, until you marry me, you are not allowed to put anything up my pussy. I didn't make up the rules. Now, go back to where you were, Athlete. Behind me.

Snorting laughter.

Silence.

Slurping kisses. The moans returned. If she could only see the lovers who made a bed out of this overgrown field, see the girl whose moans reminded her of the early mornings in her own bed back home. When the girl stood up, half her body appeared between the gaps in the grass. One kohled eye, half of her red lips, half of her chest, her dark nipple protruding like a bud. Saba saw it was Samhiya.

When Saba arrived home, Hagos was sitting on the blanket. He didn't ask where she'd been. Around him she was free. Unlike her friends back home, she had never had to report her every move to the man in the house.

At times, his silent presence in her life made Saba think he was a figment of her imagination. An ideal brother made up in the mind of a lonely child. He was perfect. And perfection didn't exist. And if it did, it was bound to shatter. Saba shuddered at the thought, quickly knelt by his side and embraced him. Soaked by her sweat, Hagos took off his shirt and lay back on the blanket, his head on his palms. From his oversized shorts protruded his long, smooth legs. Stripes of light fell on his chest. Saba stretched next to him. His bare skin smelt of jasmine fragrance. He always smelt this way, as if he was a jinni that had burst into this world out of a perfumed bottle.

Hagos kept his gaze on the ceiling. I wish I knew what you are thinking about, Saba said. She turned her face towards his, attempting to deduce an answer from it. As her eyes dwelt on him, Saba imagined him many years from now. Still alone. Time, though, moved on. The athlete and Samhiya married. With children. All the while, Hagos lay still in this camp, in this hut, on this blanket. Wrinkles had formed on his cheeks. And underneath his long eyelashes and kohled eyes, lines of exhaustion and of fatigue crammed together, clogging up his sight. He smelt of neglect, of years gone by untouched. An old, sexless, loveless, lonely Hagos trailing the youthful athlete who had taken a different path to old age, with frequent stops at several oases to replenish his soul in the arms of lovers.

Saba looked away from the scene in her mind to find Hagos's head on her shoulder. As she stroked his hair, she closed her eyes. They fell asleep like this.

Then the door opened. Its bump against the wall sent Saba jolting from her sleep. The midwife stood still, her hand holding the doorknob, their mother behind her.

Hagos turned around and continued his nap.

Do they sleep in the same blanket together?

Their mother nodded. A smile shadowed her creased lips as she said: What can we do, we didn't bring enough blankets and Saba, as you know, is a bad sleeper. My whole body aches, and I can't take extra pain from her.

The midwife shook her head. I know you are illiterate, she said to their mother. But bringing up children is not like looking after sheep. Your problem is that whatever I say goes in one ear and out the other.

The mother lowered her head, her eyes blinking.

And you? The midwife's green eyes widened at Saba. Don't you know right from wrong? What kind of education did you have at that school you loved so much?

Hagos snored. Saba envied his peace of mind. He could sleep without delay and right through the night. Even on the night the war came, he seemed unperturbed. As he was when their mother told them that she had decided they had to leave their home. He'd simply started packing straight away.

They should no longer share a bed, the midwife said, vowing that she would look for an extra blanket around the camp.

After the women left, Saba sat back on the blanket next to Hagos. When she thought of their pending separation, at her brother's loneliness by day extending to night, tears stung behind her eyelids.

That same evening, Saba went to see Samhiya. She sat on the bare wooden-framed bed held together with leather straps outside

Samhiya's hut and watched as the city girl prepared tea. Saba believed Hagos was as infatuated with her friend as the rest of the men in the camp, but because of his disability she was out of his reach. Now, Hagos's perceived obsession became hers. Saba shuffled on her stool as Samhiya bent to pour water into a pot which she had placed on top of the open furnace. Her cleavage strained the neckline of her dress and fired Saba's imagination. It was as if Saba had left her body and swarmed over Samhiya, absorbing details of the city girl from all angles, so that when Hagos would look into Saba's eyes later, he would see sketches of this desirable girl there to keep as his. Samhiya blew into the charcoals until they flared glowing red and her lips smouldered.

Samhiya's mother emerged from the hut with a comb. She sat next to Saba and called her daughter over. If you still want your hair braided, get your big bum over here, she said.

If my bum is big, said Samhiya, what do you say about Saba's?

The mother leapt to her feet and slapped her daughter on her behind.

Ouch. Mamma, stop it, said the city girl.

As Samhiya made her way to the hut, she limped, steadying herself with one hand on the wall. Saba did not understand. The slap wasn't that hard for her to be in pain like that.

Saba, can you call the midwife, Samhiya's mother said.

Samhiya paused and turned towards her mother. No, she said. No. No midwife for me, please. It's nothing. It's my foot, I twisted it on my way to the forest with Saba this morning. Isn't that true, Saba?

Saba didn't say anything.

Saba? Isn't that true?

Saba nodded. Yes, she said to her friend's mother. I urged Samhiya to be careful. But, as you know, your daughter is a risk-taker.

Okay, okay, said Samhiya, rolling her eyes at Saba. Let's say I learnt a lesson, wise girl.

Saba thought of Hagos. He had become more than the guilt she carried. Everything she did, she did for two. She spoke for two. She studied and dreamt for two. Asked questions for two. Her eyes were his, as were all her other senses. And now, as she looked at Samhiya, Saba wanted to fill the absence of passion in his life in a pragmatic way, in the

same way she fetched water to quench his thirst, brought him food from
the aid centre and spinach from the wild to feed his hunger. Just as she
filled the role of a best friend as well as a sister, she imagined it possible
that he could make love through her.

Saba sneaked in after Samhiya as her friend retreated into the hut.
She stood by the door and watched Samhiya undress, and then, pulling
down the back of her underwear, stroked the curves of her behind.

Let me help you, said Saba.

Samhiya turned and silently stared at Saba. She then hid her mouth
behind her hand and smiled.

Saba closed the door.

Saba arrived at their hut from Samhiya's breathless and woke Hagos
up from his sleep. Hagos sat up and rubbed his eyes. Saba held
him – if he could only breathe in the smell of Samhiya's skin on hers,
feel the pubic hair her tongue had touched for him, and see the shape
of Samhiya's vagina reflected in her eyes. Hagos, though, closed his eyes
and laid his head on Saba's thighs.

THE BLOOD

Saba walked to the furthest part of the open field, and once she crouched between the long, thick grass, she took off her dress. Back home, whenever they visited her uncle, who was a politician turned bandit, he would call her and Hagos to his room, and ask them to take off their tops.

You can't see who is the girl and who is the boy, he would say, his exact words repeated each visit, the same actions too. He would rub Hagos's breasts - as if he could flatten them by pushing them inward - and pull Saba's nipples harder and longer to increase her breast size.

It's for your own good, he would say. But he could never reverse God's creation. And so one day, on another trip to his town, one of the last before they fled to the camp, the uncle, professing doubt about their respective genders, asked the siblings to pull down their underwear. To make sure, he said.

That's when Saba realized that Hagos might have been born a mute, but their society turned every child into one. Her uncle knew this, and it was what made him touch them everywhere, all the time, until he decided to sleep between them. But don't worry, he told Saba, whispering his words, reassuring her that he would not spoil her future, because he would have her the same way he was going to have Hagos. Saba didn't understand. That was when he turned them both forcibly and slowly ran his hands down their backs. You are both mute now, he said to Saba and Hagos. You hear? And as he moved between them, digging, he planted more than doubts, fear, anger and pain into Saba and Hagos, he also seeded a bond between them as he scooped blood from one sibling to deposit it into the other.

TV: LIBERATION OF A MAN

S aba hadn't seen Jamal for a while and when one day three funeral
processions passed in front of her hut, all for men who had died
suddenly, Saba walked up the hill where the entertainer lived. Saba saw
a table laid out with flowers and a tape player. She was about to walk
towards Jamal's door when he came out holding his box. The TV is
back, Saba blurted out.

Jamal turned and their eyes locked. Saba smiled. She wanted to ask
him if he had brought back Dawit and the Signorina from the dead
to continue their forbidden love story. Jamal didn't say anything as he
placed the box on the table, but Saba caught a fleeting smile on his face
as she walked over and sat on a chair facing the cardboard.

Jamal began narrating. Today's show is called: The Last Liberation:
The Way a Man Wants to Make Love. He slipped his cardboard character
into the TV from the hole at the top. The male character stood next to a
Vespa against a drawing of Africa. He was holding a bag.

Saba noticed a mysterious smile on the face of the man about to
journey across the continent, as Jamal narrated, for someone who can
love him the way he is and make love in the way he wants.

Jamal turned on the tape player. Soft, sensual Ethiopian music accompanied the man's lonely travels on his Vespa. Then the man stopped and began to talk, imagining he had found a woman with whom he could be free, showing her how music inhabited his bones.

He rocked, softly shaking his shoulders, talking to this woman. He put his hands on his knees and swayed his from hips side to side, going low and rising high, as if surfing on waves of her lust.

Saba gasped, her pulse quickened. She unbuttoned her dress and drew breath from the man who was now in Niger. When Saba clapped, the man undressed. He tucked his penis between his legs. I am more than just a penis. Sometimes, I want to make love with my

Heart
Imagination
Dreams
History
Story
Eyes
Breathing you in whole
Hearing you talk all night long
Washing you
Shaving you
Sinking into your sweaty armpits
Gagging on your tongue
Watching you as you work, dream, walk, study, rage, cry, laugh
Hearing you moan
I want to orgasm by eating your orgasm.

Jamal dropped the character and entered his hut. The yearning lover fell on the ground. Saba picked him up and held him close, his head between her breasts.

The music stopped.

THE NEW BLANKET

Saba had arrived at the apartment built by their grandmother whistling a song. She was holding a letter from her teacher which commended her for another top mark, and a pack of Hagos's favourite sweets which she had bought to thank him for doing all the chores while she studied. Her thick braids, which he had styled for her the evening before, framed her face like a crown. Saba was about to open the gate when she heard the midwife screaming abuse at her mother. Saba climbed the wall and peered inside their stone-floored courtyard. Her mother stood in front of the midwife, head down. Behind the two women the door to Saba's room was open. Hagos sat next to the terracotta pots full of herbs cooking Saba's dinner. She smelt the fried lamb with shoro that she liked to have on the last evening of her school week. The flowers their grandmother planted against the wall for her lover living on the other side quivered in the afternoon breeze.

Saba put the letter and pack of sweets in her school bag and rushed straight past the two women to her room. She closed the door.

Saba, come out now.

Give me one minute, Adday, Saba said. I need to change.

Saba slipped out of her school uniform and checked her underwear, wondering if perhaps she'd become a woman, with her mother having noticed first in the laundry basket. But normally Hagos washed their clothes, and she was sure he would have showed it to her, not to her mother. There was no blood, so no interruption of her studies. Saba clenched her fist and smiled.

Saba rubbed some cream her brother had made all over her legs. Her smooth thighs glistened. Ignoring the waiting women, Saba began to prepare for her evening studies. She arranged her books across one side of her bed, placing her pens and notebooks next to her pillow, leaving the side next to the wall free. Smiling and smelling of rosemary and thyme, Saba emerged, dressed in her black nightgown.

With Saba inside the living room, the mother closed the door.

Don't worry. I will expel her demons, the midwife said to the mother. Then she lit the charcoal, and instead of normal frankincense gum, she used berbere spice.

Saba knew the type of punishment about to come, she had had a few of them already, all when she'd disobeyed her mother. Like a few months earlier, when her mother had asked Saba to do the chores instead of Hagos, because people were talking.

So what? Saba had responded. We are both happy, why can you not just let it be?

The midwife pulled Saba by the arm. Come and sit here.

What have I done to deserve this? the mother cried. God, why have you given me a mute son and a daughter who is deaf to me?

She was made to sit in a chair. As her mother sobbed, she tried to guess her crime this time. Perhaps it had to do with her studies, for which she isolated herself in her room day and night, as she worked to achieve the results she needed for a scholarship to the university. But it could have also been because her mother had walked in on her while she was masturbating a few days before.

The berbere smoke coiled towards the ceiling fan which had hung still ever since the generator left by their grandmother had been taken by the dergue. Since then Saba had to study by candlelight or by the light of the oil lamp.

Saba coughed as she undressed. She waited for the cover to be thrown over her head, the burner with chilli to be placed between her legs, so that her bad spirits would burn in the smoke. It had always amazed Saba how her mother and the midwife thought of her traits as though they were aliens who'd come to reside inside her that they could chase away with fire. But Saba had chosen to be this way, stubborn, focused, unrelenting in her pursuit of excellence. She was proud of the trait these two women kept accusing her of as if it was an insult: being manly.

But then, and to her horror, the midwife knelt in front of Saba and parted her legs, peering closely. How could you lie to me? she asked, shaking Saba's mother. Why didn't you do it?

Saba's mother trembled, looking away from the midwife.

Who will take your daughter as a wife now? The midwife emptied the jar of berbere onto the incense burner.

It was her grandmother, the mother said. She vowed she would cut my head if I ever touched Saba.

Go and get me a razor now, the midwife demanded.

Saba's mother didn't move.

The midwife cast a blanket over both the incense holder and Saba.

Did you not hear what I said? This explains why Saba is different to all the other girls I have delivered. Oh Lord, I ask your forgiveness.

Between the coughs, the sharp pains in her chest, the unbearable smell, Saba wondered what this thing was that had enraged the midwife. What did the midwife see between her thighs that drove her to fury?

The world turned dark, though it burst into flames again as the blanket touched the charcoal and caught fire. And so did Saba's thighs.

Saba turned her eyes away from the thatched roof, from the memory. As she turned to pick up the blanket given to her by the midwife, Saba felt dizzy. She leaned against the pole and closed her eyes. Memories that don't fade away with time and distance are the ones written on your skin.

Since the midwife couldn't find a spare blanket anywhere in the camp, she gave hers to Saba. The woman used her gabi as a bed, downgrading her comfort to separate Saba from her brother. But no one will, Saba vowed, remembering that night – her brother's fingers and hers intertwining as their uncle knelt behind them.

No one will, Saba vowed again as she placed the midwife's blanket against the wall between Hagos and her mother.

Saba and Zahra were strolling around the camp. The imam announced the evening prayer from the makeshift mosque bordered with red rocks. Kids ran around. Roasted coffee beans wafted in the air. Hold me, said Saba.

I thought you didn't like to be that close, said Zahra.

Sometimes I do, said Saba.

You are moody, said Zahra. Just like me.

They laughed and held hands.

Saba?

Yes.

Can I be honest?

Saba paused and nodded. Yes.

Sometimes, your silence disturbs me, said Zahra. I mean, your brother's is natural, but yours feels forced.

Saba didn't say anything.

I worry about you.

Don't, said Saba. It's the sardines. My breath smells of fish. So I keep quiet.

I'm serious, said Zahra. Have you always been like this?

Zahra, how long have we been here?

You see what I mean? You are trying to change the subject.

Zahra glanced down at the watch on her wrist that had belonged to her mother. It will record the time passing, her mother had said before going to the front. So you know that there will come a time when we are together again. But the battery of the watch had died and now time stood still on Zahra's wrist. Zahra had manipulated the watch so the two hands stood together, embracing. The mother and daughter inseparable in time, if not in place.

It doesn't matter, said Saba, pulling Zahra's hand. They continued their walk, zigzagging through the crowd to avoid people sitting in groups, others cooking. Milk spilled from a pot onto the open furnace. I love the smell of milk on charcoal, said Saba.

You are strange, said Zahra.

I never denied that, said Saba, grinning.

What a smile, said a man to Saba, standing in front of her.

Just keep walking, said Zahra to the man.

Can someone ration humour to this girl? said the man to those around him.

And can anyone ration him a brain? said Zahra, spitting.

The man was held back by his friends and the girls hurried down the pathway. I will get you, the man shouted at Zahra.

He'll probably get into another argument in a second and forget about us, said Zahra. Anyway, my grandmother is waiting to listen to my mother's tape. Come with me.

THE SECOND-HAND CLOTHES

Ululations seeped into the hut. Saba peered through the window. A woman had delivered a baby. Saba didn't know whether the woman had arrived pregnant or conceived in the camp. The passage of time she had tried to ignore was sharpening its blade.

A convoy of a Land Rover trailed by a few lorries made its way to the aid centre. Zahra appeared from behind the cloud of dust, grabbing Saba by her hand.

Where have you been? Saba asked. Zahra, how is it possible we do not see each other for a long time in this small place?

To be seen and seeing each other are not the same, Zahra said, smiling. She pointed to the lorries. Come on, let's go and look. Maybe they will be the ones to build our school.

By now, Saba thought, she should have been in college, the gates of university within sight. How long have we been here? Zahra took her friend by the arm and ran to the aid centre.

A man with a briefcase climbed down from the Land Rover. The aid supplier, as he was called by staff, greeted the aid coordinator and handed him a newspaper.

The Englishman held the newspaper open in front of him, his eyes sparkling with every page he turned. It was as if the stories from back home soothed his loneliness.

The Khwaja filed past Saba and Zahra and engaged in a conversation with the Englishman. Both men bent their heads over the newspaper, the Khwaja nodding his head as the Englishman talked. The Englishman gesticulated, the smile across his face turning into laughter, as if memories had lifted off the mask he wore in the camp and revealed another version of him.

The Englishman handed the paper to the Khwaja, who hurried home without stopping to pick up his share of the second-hand clothes the aid workers were instructed to distribute to the refugees.

Boss, just like that? said one of the staff from the back of a lorry to the aid supplier. Shouldn't we at least ask for their sizes?

So you think we should line up all these refugees, measure them up and then sort out all these clothes according to gender and size? the aid supplier asked. Maybe we should also consider their individual taste? Just throw the clothes off the lorry.

They did. Saba looked up. For a moment, everything was suspended in the air. Shirts, jeans, underwear, dresses and bras flew above people's heads. Clothes and underclothes, the public and the private, all mingled in the free air before they fell to earth, where separation began, where humanity had to be divided into sections, as if that was the only way to live. Even in this wilderness, boundaries mattered.

I have a dress, she heard a man yelling. Anyone with trousers or a shirt?

A woman called out: Anyone with children's clothing? I have adult clothes for my boy.

Saba, though, held on to a brown T-shirt and a long pair of mauve trousers that fell in front of her, and looked for Hagos among the crowd in search of something that fitted. She found him with a girl's dress. He was about to leave when Saba caught his hand. Wait, Hagos, she said. I'll help you exchange your dress for men's clothes.

Hagos looked down, and Saba felt she understood why.

Back in their hut, Saba put the clothes inside her jute sack, instead preferring her old black dress. The British newspaper, though, stayed in her mind.

When she arrived at the Khwaja's, he had fallen asleep in a chair outside his hut, the British newspaper in his lap. Mosquitoes buzzed by the oil lamp he had placed on a tree trunk table next to him.

The Khwaja opened his eyes and stretched out his arms.

The English call this a power nap. An apt description, indeed. Take a seat, my dear, he said to Saba.

He pointed to a large expired sardine box turned upside down.

Excusing himself, the Khwaja returned to his reading. He rocked in his chair, laughing, once in a while nodding in agreement with the writer of the piece: That's right. That's right.

You have more energy than I do, said Saba. I feel as expired as this box you make me sit on.

The Khwaja laughed. Saba, you have a dry sense of humour. You would get along well with these people. He tapped faces on the paper with the back of his hand.

The pages ruffled in the breeze. Saba stretched her neck and noticed a picture of a girl in a black gown, beaming under a square cap.

She has become a doctor, the Khwaja said. But the article is about her future. As a woman, she will earn a lot less than a male doctor.

Where did she study? Saba asked.

Saba, haven't you heard what I said? The same education, but lower earnings. That's scandalous. And they call themselves civilized.

The smiling girl on the page creased under his enraged fist, falling like a judge's gavel. The girl now appeared to share the Khwaja's anger. Her face frowned. Saba took the newspaper and ironed out the Khwaja's frustrations from the graduate's face.

The graduate and Saba exchanged a quick glance under the moonlight of the camp. One day, I want to go to her university, Saba said. Can you teach me English?

The Khwaja looked up at Saba.

She wasn't smiling.

The morning sun burned on her back as Saba took her pail and headed to the river. The priest read from his book. Worshippers closed their eyes, as if they were searching for the god inside them.

Outside the camp, Saba encountered a group of men who parted and stood on each side of the narrow path to let her pass.

The walls of men shuffled towards each other. Her hips bounced against their bodies, in a swing she was unaccustomed to. Saba is transformed into a dancing beauty, one of the men said, laughing.

Another grabbed her hair, halting her march.

He buried his nose into her neck, lamenting the length of time since he had smelt the fragrance of a woman's skin.

Saba was sure she smelt exactly as him, as them. She was sweating too. It appeared odd to her that even in this camp, a woman in these men's minds remained unblemished. Womanhood uplifted, endlessly floating above the harshness of reality, untouched by tragedy.

The other men brought their noses closer to take in this womanly scent.

Saba let out a fart.

The wall of men collapsed and Saba sprinted to the river.

An announcement came through a megaphone. The English aid coordinator spoke, his assistant translated. Now that we have distributed clothes, doctors will come tomorrow, for quick check-ups.

And the doctors came, as he promised. But by the time they had finished seeing the long queue of children, dusk had fallen. Saba's mother, queuing with the midwife, was seen late at night. Most patients were made to take the same pill, like the sardines, the same-sized huts, the air they breathed, the river water they drank, this single pill that was meant to cure all their ailments.

But many, like Saba and Hagos, towards the end of the queue, weren't seen by the doctors. Next time, the aid coordinator promised. The doctors will come back soon, God willing.

Even the Englishman learnt to evoke God in everything he said.

DISGUST IS AN
ACQUIRED TASTE

The family of three sat to eat dinner.
Three silences.

Hers.

Her brother's.

Her mother's.

They were empty of things to say to each other. And Saba wondered how the camp took one's language too as if it was flesh attached to bones. She could visualize the haemorrhaging of her words, everyone's words. No one without a language is alive.

Saba lay in her blanket and was awake when footsteps tapered into silence.

She left the hut. Lately, she had started walking around the camp by night. Saba felt less impatient then. The horizon that she scanned by day, that open sunlit bright space that stretched into infinity, the empty space she filled with her dreams, that space was reduced to nothing at night.

Life, and all its possibilities, became obscured by darkness. And night offered her freedom by giving her invisibility from herself (from the coloured wound on her thighs), from men, from the midwife, from her mother who inspected her for signs of puberty, from her brother who sought her body as a blackboard for a language he lacked.

Night was a better time to live in the camp, Saba decided. It was also when she masturbated in the open toilet, where she orgasmed as well as urinated and defecated.

Saba inhaled her orgasm. It had the smell of her insides. A garden. The garden of climbing flowers her grandmother had planted to break through the barrier separating her from her lover, full of pepper plants, lemon trees and that sour tasty orange. Saba smuggled this garden, the desires that bloomed every spring with the flowers, into the camp in her womb, without her mother watching, and without the smuggler, who charged for every single item, ever finding out.

The chirping of crickets filled her ears. Now and then, howls rose out of the bush. And petered out. Saba sauntered across the square. She noticed a shadow against a wall behind her. It was the same silhouette that followed her on most of her recent walks. The tall black figure with a yellow flat cap who glided on the mud walls behind her. She suspected it was Jamal.

He was her shadow by night. Silent. He was her dark side, never visible in daylight. She knew more than he supposed.

Saba entered the field. When she crouched, her toes, long, unfiled nails, appeared in the light of her torch. The hair on her legs had grown. Her dry skin itched. Her curls had returned. Since she stayed awake by night, and away from Hagos's care, wildness returned to her. Her guilt slept with Hagos.

Wind blew through the field. Long grass whipped against her and Saba lowered her head and examined the map of her thighs. Her pubic bones protruded like columns guarding a monument. But Saba quickly freed her thoughts and language from the corset of decency that imprisoned her body parts in politeness. She pushed her clitoris back and forth against the dark lips of her vagina. Between her legs she saw a hand that rustled through the dry grass. Fingers clasped into a knot, holding a handkerchief. Saba shivered as the cool hand rested against her inner thighs before reaching further, further towards the skin she usually scraped at with stones.

It was on one of her walkabouts – as she strode among the night moths and clouds of insects, pausing now and then against a hut, listening to beds creaking under the weight of tenderness or restless sleepers – that Saba discovered, located in the east of the camp, a woman called Azyeb who had turned her hut into a bar selling suwa.

Saba switched off her torch and sat behind a thick shrub at the side of Azyeb's hut. She held on to the privilege of invisibility. The odour of fermented beer and sounds of laughter wafted through the air. The athlete and Jamal sat opposite each other next to empty stools in the light slanting from the hut's window. A three-stone stove in the middle, the fire shimmering. Smoke twisted in front of them.

Azyeb emerged from her hut behind a short man, buttoning up her blouse. Saba recognized the praise poet. He had become known around the camp not for his poetry but for forcing his wife to eat his share of the aid meals. He loved his women plump. Although the real reason was different, the joke went around that his wife requested a divorce when her malnourished husband couldn't function in bed any more.

Azyeb sat down on her stool and lit a cigarette on the stove. Taking a long drag, she sighed. I needed that, she said.

The smoke of a satisfied woman reached Saba. The faces of the three men appeared and disappeared in the flickering light. Conversations between them and the barwoman flew back and forth over beer. Saba overheard it all, and when she went home that night she took with her what was said about Hagos.

And when Saba and Hagos sat down for breakfast, the dialogue of the night before replayed in her mind: Poor man. He is older than us, said the praise poet. His mother has been looking for a wife for him. But no girl, I mean even the poorest or the ugliest, would take an illiterate mute for a husband.

But how do you know it is the girls and not the parents who reject him? said Azyeb. Since when do girls have a say about who they marry anyway? Perhaps things would be different if we did.

Saba looked at Hagos. His hair covered his ears now. He ate like her mother. Fingers turned into an elegant spoon, his chewing inaudible. He was the girl her mother had always wanted.

You are growing fast, the midwife had said to Saba some time ago. One day soon, a nice man will walk into this hut with a ring. Since then, Saba had begun to imagine herself at her wedding, in her husband's bed, a certain time in a future when she was surrounded by her own children, while Hagos remained in this blanket, in this hut, old, lonely, childless. Dying without ever experiencing love.

Saba tucked his hair behind his ears. She hushed the flies away. She found it strange that Hagos was twenty-something and had yet to grow a moustache or beard. That was a miracle. God ought to be thanked for Hagos's eternal youth, she thought. There was still time. Love was bound to find its way to him.

Saba wiped the grains of sleep from the corners of her brother's eyes. Hagos smiled. But Saba yearned for a conversation now, something else between them rather than silence. Smiles no longer had the same weight. They faded against the urge to talk, to exchange jokes, to scream. Screaming at him, for rejecting her pleas to teach him to read and write for all those years.

Perhaps, Saba thought, they ought to play the game they used to play. A game that started when the Paris-educated landlord and photographer had told Saba and Hagos that a picture said more than a thousand words. Then, Saba had wanted Hagos to take as many pictures of her as possible. So she could know his thoughts about her, his feelings towards her. She'd wanted him to talk to her this way, instead of having to rely on guesswork, on her endless interpretations of his actions. Saba no longer wanted to be an interpreter. She wanted to sit back and listen to him.

As if he could read her mind, Hagos had made a fake camera using a tin can. Saba's poses, though, were real. Hagos had stood behind his tin camera, beginning a dialogue.

Now, as she sat in front of him in their hut, Saba recalled some of the pictures he'd taken. Their meanings became clearer with the distance of time and place. And Saba, the resident of the camp, could remember without a hint of remorse or shame the time he fiddled with her cheek, nose, eyes, until he had scrunched her up. The time he braided her hair into a bun and crossed one of her legs over the other, his hands opening the buttons of her dress, his cold skin on her chest, her breasts exposed to this photographer peering through the hole in the tin. The picture he took after he kohled her eyes, and then wet her eyelashes, remained in her mind as vividly as it would have done had he taken an actual picture. Saba's body bore his dejections, his happiness, dreams and desires.

Saba wondered if he'd brought the tin camera with him, to continue the conversation in this place.

Later that night, Saba lay on her side, her head on her arm, watching a sleeping Hagos. His face glowed next to the dimmed oil lamp she put by his side. Saba could hear the rain splattering against the roof. The wind falling like blows on the mud wall. On a night like this, her senses heightened. The world was about to fall. And not just hers. The praise poet's words from the day before came again to Saba: Poor Hagos, he will die a virgin.

Saba stood up and prepared to wash herself. She undressed and turned up the wick of the lamp. Her chest, torso, thighs and legs all came alive, unburying her from the darkness. Hagos opened his eyes. And closed them again.

Saba stepped out of the bucket and shuffled to Hagos's jute sack. Knowing she should not, she still went ahead and broke the oath, and for the first time since they arrived at the camp, she opened the sack. She slipped her hand inside and rummaged through his belongings folded and stacked away. Underneath a shirt, a pair of trousers and some shorts, there was a plastic bag. On opening it, an intense aroma burst out. Hagos had packed Indian oil for skin and hair. Perfumed acacia. Sandalwood for incense-bathing. A jar of caramelized sugar wax. Dilka, the perfumed exfoliate.

Saba put aside Hagos's collection of aromatic bottles and searched further. A leather bag at the bottom of the jute sack caught her interest. Inside, she found a set of colouring pencils and a stack of papers wrapped in a black lace scarf. A discovery in the middle of the pile distracted her from her thoughts. There it was, the nude painting gifted to her by the landlord. For years it had hung on the wall of her room back home. Saba had wanted to take it with her when they fled, but feared it would not fit in a camp. Yet Hagos had brought it.

Saba brought the familiar painting of a woman taking a bath, somewhere in Paris, closer to her face. We meet again, my dear, she mumbled. How much I missed you.

Saba blew the dust off her one-time roommate. The warm air bounced off the painting. Their naked skins touched. Heat, sweet memories, shelved desires sank into her pores. Saba rubbed her inner thighs, inserting a finger inside herself. A cockroach slithered from underneath her and climbed her brother's legs.

RICE

One morning, lorries drove into the camp with more provisions. As well as oil and sugar, they brought sacks of rice to distribute to the residents of the camp.

We would have preferred pasta, if you'd asked us, the praise poet said.

Saba laughed.

We can't help it, sir, said the praise poet. The Italians are to blame.

Saba walked up to the aid coordinator and asked about school.

One day, soon, said the Eritrean man standing next to the Englishman. First, eat, be healthy, and then school will come.

God willing.

THE COMMITTEE OF ELDERS

Saba opened the door of her hut onto the square. She raised a hand against the sun. The judge and the men making up the committee of elders stood in front of a crowd.

Days before she left their hometown, her teacher – a woman who had said she was a direct descendant of the Queen of Sheba, not in blood but in power – comforted her that a new place always offered a new beginning and a fresh start.

But what would her teacher have made of the judge staging another moral trial which, he explained, helped retain cultural values and entrench tradition in this place in the wilderness?

Back home, the judge said through his megaphone, I presided over many cases that highlighted to me the dark sides of our humanity. I fought them there and I will do so here even more. Today, the moral trial was aimed at stray unmarried girls who... He paused, as if searching for the appropriate words. Saba completed his sentence to herself: Girls who discovered how to enjoy the same pleasure as boys without destroying their marriage prospects.

Saba wondered whether it had been Samhiya who was caught, but it was another girl, who was found in the bush, her dress lifted up to her waist. She sat in the front of the eager spectators. The trial, which was more like a public re-enacting of the crime, started.

The girl with plaited hair and a cross tattooed on her forehead stood in front of the heavily built man she was accused of seducing. The man turned away from her and ran to his wife in the audience: Forgive me, he said to his wife, surrounded by their children.

The judge ordered the man to come back and when he did, the girl's mother rushed forward and screamed: My daughter did not seduce this man. He raped her.

But the girl's father scurried towards his wife and slapped her. It's your fault for letting her wear this. Against his body he held the dress his daughter wore that night: Just look, he said.

On the instruction of the judge the girl was taken away to a nearby hut and returned wearing the dress, which barely covered her knees.

The judge read out a statement with a verdict: Impurity will be rooted out from this camp. We will not allow this wilderness to corrupt our souls. This girl will bear her sin on her back.

The man climbed on the back of his seducer. And the girl trudged around the square carrying the man, her sin, an adult double her size.

The girl's back bent. Yet, Saba noticed, she didn't flinch. She didn't wince. Girls, she thought, are used to carrying things: firewood, water, food for their families, their brothers and sisters, mothers and fathers, as well as themselves and their own sorrows. No amount of weight can crush a girl.

But Saba also knew that this girl's real punishment was the reputation inflicted on her. From now on, she would be confined to the backroom of life, to a place where she would be forgotten, like a building left alone to decay, so that when a man drove past and sought shelter in her body as a last resort, in his drunken hour, he would find her infested with rats, bats, spiders, mites. This girl, Saba thought, would be a moral ghost story for generations to come.

S aba turned the wick down and leaned against the wall. There had been a storm that night, and the rain that began when Saba lay down on her blanket hadn't stopped. She brought her legs up against her chest. Humid air seeped through the cracks in the window and the door.

The rain outside intensified, dispersing the warm air inside the hut. Hagos wrapped his arms around himself. He used to hold her as they slept. There were moments when Saba would wake up in the middle of the night to find her legs embraced by his arms. His cheek resting on her feet. A smile on his face.

She heard the rumbling of the sky, the hissing wind, and saw a flash of lightning through the window. She imagined the thatch stripped off the roof, the rain leaking through. Her head above the water, so she could hardly breathe.

She fell asleep with that thought, with the feeling of suffocation, her head leaning against the wall. And when she woke up some time later, both her mother and her brother were still asleep. Her blanket was dry, though her underwear was wet.

The next morning was sweltering, the breeze heavy with moisture. Little heaps of dry mud dotted the square, and the red rocks of the mosque were covered in sand, the outline of the mosque obscured, once again. God is everywhere, Saba repeated to herself, recalling the imam's words on that first morning.

She was on her way to the river, barefoot. As she looked at her toes covered in mud, Saba felt that her dress had shrunk, travelling up on her growing legs, stretched by her widening hips. Her knees were visible. It seemed miraculous to her that she was still growing, while feeding on sardines and the powdered milk and rice that had arrived only recently.

Saba walked with firm steps. The muscles in her calves pressed her feet down. She left permanent footprints. This was her wilderness. She entered the damp narrow path that led to the river. A path like a black viper slithering between the grass, pushing against the cactuses and thorny shrubs. A lizard crept from underneath a rock. An old man came down the slightly sloping land from the opposite direction. He walked unaided, his gait youthful, his age visible only in his wrinkles and eyes that squinted to fit what was worth observing around him. The old man paused. Good morning, bella, he said.

Saba stopped. She stared at her shadow on the path, the outline of the bucket against the grass. Why are shadows always dark? she thought, recalling the time her landlord back home took her to his studio and showed her the negatives of the pictures he was developing. Then he came behind her in the darkroom and squeezed her waist and Saba discovered that everyone has a dark side.

The old man came closer, their shadows merging on the long, dry grass. You might not know it, he said to Saba, but I have been watching you ever since we arrived. My lady, you have grown beautifully.

A lady? The future had caught up with her while she stood in the same place. She had deemed time irrelevant, because it was as infinite as the air. But time moved even if everything else in the camp remained static.

The man reached his hand to her face. He caressed away a strand of her hair. We are lucky, it is a quiet morning, he said, stroking the side of her arm.

He pointed to the field, to the natural bed, wild grass, roasting sand, wet rocks teeming with insects. The old man took her hand but Saba didn't move.

People have confused being a refugee with the end of life, he said. They have mistaken being in a camp with being inside a graveyard. We are human beings. We have our needs wherever we are. But I shouldn't blame you all. I am not young and have suffered the misfortune of war and exile a few times already. I have learned never to leave my desires behind me in the ruins.

The grass around them shook. For a moment, she felt like an animal trapped. His pulse that pounded on her wrist calmed. The old man released her hand. I want a woman to be alive in my arms, he said.

And then he was gone.

She ran up the hill, past the trees, over shrubs, along the valley, zigzagging on another narrow passage, before she sprinted down the slope all the way to the bank of the river. There, she chose a quiet spot and perched on a small stone. Cool water lapped against her shins. There were a few girls scattered along the bank in the far distance to her right washing clothes. Heads bowed. Hands scrubbing.

Saba rubbed her underwear with scentless soap. Her hands weakened for a moment and the river current tugged away her piece of clothing. She threw herself into the water and swam further into the river. Holding her breath, she dived.

From the river, Saba walked deep into the bush and climbed to the top of an acacia tree, spreading her dress on the branches around her. She sat on another branch until it dried. She unwrapped her arms from around her chest, freeing her breasts. The hair under her arms was as long as the dense bush between her legs. She recalled the old man's warning.

Don't make the mistake I did when the first war found me when I was young and took suffering to heart, he said. Life is for living even if you are far away from home.

THE BUSINESSMAN

Saba was woken from sleep by the roar of engines. She followed Hagos out of the hut as dozens of lorries made their way into the camp and parked in a row. The square lit up as though it was daytime. A crowd gathered. Saba's gaze darted over the dust-covered faces on the back of the lorries.

Unlike the previous occasion, when Saba and the current camp's residents had arrived at this place, there was little weeping. The newcomers sat still on the back of the lorries. Heads dropped low. A woman near Saba raised her voice, asking: Why are you here? We hoped the war would be over. We hoped to make our way back instead of receiving you here.

We did not come here from our country, said a man, leaning over the frame of his lorry. We have been living in this country for years, but the authorities evicted us from the city early this morning without warning. We didn't even have time to say goodbyes. They sent the army to our houses at dawn and now we are here.

He wept.

Attention. Attention, a voice came through a megaphone.

Saba looked up at the speaker standing on top of a lorry's cabin, wearing dark glasses and white jellabiya, with a white imma wound around his head, Kalashnikov slung over his shoulder. Attention drivers, said the man. Lorries can't pass through the lanes to the east of the camp where these refugees need to go to. Drop them here and let them sort out the final metres themselves.

Drivers banged on the sides of their lorries: Come down. Hurry up.

Why the hurry? Saba wondered, recalling the way their driver, Tahir, had helped them.

The new refugees unloaded their belongings. Bed frames. Rolled-up mattresses. Cupboards. Tables. Chairs. Plastic flowers and plants. Sacks of fruit. Part of the city descended on the camp, carried on the backs of women and men whose lives had been interrupted earlier that morning to be dropped here, as though they were things.

An old man with a tape measure around his neck stood next to a foot-operated sewing machine fixed on top of a table, a half-sewn dress still under its needle.

A balding man with a sign – Barber of Taka Mountain – disembarked next. Further down the line, Saba saw a woman stepping out of the cab of the lorry in a silky black dress and red high heels. She stood and watched as a bed, a mattress, a wardrobe, three pieces of luggage and a turquoise beauty case were placed on the heads of men who followed as she swung her way into a dark alleyway leading to the east of the camp.

By the next morning, word had gone around that a father and his son had been allocated three huts between them. Saba joined the crowd that had gathered in protest around the huts. Two were adjacent to each other, and a third, the largest, was a few metres to the right, at the foot of a steep hill where Jamal lived. Here low shrubs with little distance between them were scattered about. Red soil stretched all the way up the hill with overgrown grass to where Jamal stood watching in front of his hut.

A woman next to Saba spat in the direction of the biggest hut. They came with three lorries, she said, rocking the child tied to her back. I saw them unload last night. I can tell from the beds, the furniture and the number of boxes they brought that they are rich.

This explains it then, said the athlete. If you have money you can buy anything. Even three huts for two people.

But why would anyone with money come to a camp if they had the chance to buy off officials back in the city? Saba asked.

Curse on them, the woman said, drowning out Saba's question. Six of us, me, my husband and our four children, live in one hut.

Let's throw them out now, the athlete said.

The judge arrived in time to stop the athlete and his group of friends from carrying out the threat. We have been in this camp for a long time, the judge said. And suspicion festers in isolation. We must reserve judgement until we know all the facts.

Saba noticed a glow under the door of the largest hut. Jazz music poured out. The door opened and a young bare-chested man came out wearing only shorts. Papa vieni fuori adesso.

The music stopped.

We came to greet you, said the judge, shaking the father's hand. Welcome to our camp. It is a simple place but we have safety and sometimes that is all you need to reflect on life and its purpose. If you need anything, everyone present here would be happy to help.

Saba followed the eyes of the tall, broad-shouldered man as he inspected the crowd. He was wearing a blue robe with a spotted silk scarf knotted around his neck. He smiled and strode back inside the hut and shut the door. Then he turned the music back on.

Saba lay on her blanket with her hands behind her head and stared at the thatched roof, thinking about the father and son in their three huts. Sweat rolled down from her underarms. Hagos arrived holding wild flowers. He sat next to his sister and turned up the wick of her lamp, his eyes shining against the flame as he leaned towards her. He showed her his own hairless armpits.

Hagos, I do like it when you shave and look after yourself, but I prefer to be the way I am.

Hagos didn't say anything.

I am like a wild animal, she said. She made a growling sound and curled her hand into a claw, mimicking a lion.

She laughed.

Silence.

Are you upset with me, Hagos? Saba asked.

Hagos shook his head. And then nodded in confirmation.

You are trying to confuse me, she said. Is that a yes or a no?

Hagos chuckled and kissed Saba on her cheek. He then rubbed flower petals between her fingers.

Put some here, Saba said, pointing to his long neck. Actually, let me do it for you.

Hagos tilted his head to the side. Magic, Saba exclaimed as she perfumed his neck.

Some time later, Saba perched on a stool behind the open furnace and made tea for her mother and the midwife. The women were full of mirth as they reminisced about the days they cooked chicken stew every Sunday.

I miss that life, said the mother.

I remember, said the midwife. Even my husband preferred your chicken. God bless his soul.

Saba served tea to her mother and the midwife without looking at them and sat back on her stool. The square bathed in the silver light of the moon.

I used to make the best butter, Saba's mother said, recalling how the landlord she worked for would even bring her minced beef so she could marinate his meat in her spicy butter. He loved kitfo made my way, she said.

That man, said the midwife. He had money but no morals. The Europeans emptied him of everything our culture instilled in him. Let's hope that Eyob is different. I pray to the Lord that he is a man of God.

Who is Eyob? asked Saba's mother.

That man who came with his son last night, said the midwife. Apparently he is self-made. He owned shops and a transport business back home. He also had a hotel in Addis Ababa, but that and everything he owned was confiscated by the dergue, curse on them.

A businessman! Saba only realized she had yelled out when her mother told her to be quiet. She turned away with a smile.

This tea tastes of home, said the midwife.

Hagos taught Saba how to make it, said the mother. God bless him.

He's a blessed boy, said the midwife.

Saba drew her stool nearer to the women. Sipping on her tea, the midwife carried on speaking: Apparently Eyob opened a shop in the city before he lost that one too when he was forced to move to our camp with his son, Tedros.

Poor man, said Saba's mother, shaking her head.

Don't worry about him, said the midwife. I heard he brought with him some of his stock. He will be fine.

The following morning, Saba arrived in the deserted square, firewood tied to her back. She paused when she saw the new arrival standing in front of the makeshift aid centre. The businessman looked around him. Saba wondered whether he was prospecting the area, looking for a spot to start his business all over again. The frown that had sat between her eyebrows all morning disappeared.

When the businessman turned around, their eyes met. But Saba lost sight of him as soon as the square filled with people who made clouds of dust rise everywhere. Saba shuffled the weight of the wood from her back and, hunching forward, she whistled on her way home.

Inside the hut, she untied her ponytail. Running her fingers down the back of her neck, she raised her hair high. Sweat trickled down to her nape. With the businessman's arrival, she could see the camp transformed. Months from now, she imagined the square as a replica of her hometown market. Shops dotted along two sides facing each other. Fresh vegetables and fruits ripening in the sun. A butcher's knife wedging the meat in portions. Traders selling chickens hanging upside down from sticks on Fridays and Sundays. Clothes of the latest fashion swinging from a hanging rack outside a boutique. Women selling henna and perfume, or braiding hair.

And Saba was queuing for the weekly ration when Eyob and Tedros marched into the square carrying boxes. The son caught her eye. The cardigan tied around his neck reminded her of Jamal's puppet actor, Dawit. The father and son stopped on a dry spot, a cracked patch fed with the sweat of those who waited under the sun for food aid. They set up their makeshift market stall.

We have coffee beans, Tedros said, opening boxes. Come closer, ladies and gentlemen, and look at what we brought you from our beloved country.

He took out a jar. Our country hasn't forgotten you, he said. Come, taste it, let this honey dissolve the bitterness of exile in your veins.

The crowd around the improvised shop swelled. Saba watched from the side as people shoved and pushed each other to get near this piece of their country. Eyob and his son were squeezed out, their goods left unattended. Saba ducked when the businessman pulled out a handgun from his side pocket and shot into the air.

Four times.

I can still hear them ringing in my ears, said the midwife to the judge later, as the case was discussed by the committee of elders. How could he do this to us after we escaped violence to come here?

Let's all calm down, the judge said.

No, said the athlete. You must deal with this man now before he kills someone, or we will throw him out of the camp.

Saba imagined the businessman being chased away, the change she envisaged him bringing to the camp disappearing with him. She left the gathering and headed to the businessman's hut, even though the judge had warned them against approaching him until the court had passed its verdict.

Eyob was sitting on a chair outside the door to his hut, his eyes shut. Saba stepped closer. He had a round face with a pointy chin. Incisions on his left eyebrow reminded her of her grandmother, who had had eye problems that had to be treated this way. His short hair was greying in parts. Despite his presumed wealth, Saba found that there was a contained manner about the way he sat. Shoulders hunched, hands folded on his lap, legs pressed together. She wondered if he was still traumatized at having gone from living in a villa to a hut, from the city to a camp, from owning a business empire to being just another refugee.

The door behind the businessman opened and his son came out of the hut and stopped in the middle of a stretching movement when his eyes caught hers. Hey you. What do you want? he asked.

Saba recalled his melodic voice at the makeshift stall. His angry tone now slightly took the edge off his appeal.

Without answering him, Saba turned towards the businessman, now awake. He chased away the flies swarming around him and greeted Saba as if he was behind a counter of a shop. How may I help you, Signorina?

I saw you struggling as you tried selling in the square, Saba said, and I thought you might need an assistant.

We don't want any now, Tedros said. But we will need men to help us unload the boxes that we will import from the city as soon as we open a shop in this camp.

A shop? When are you opening it?

What's your name? Eyob asked.

Saba pictured herself standing behind the counter of the first shop in the camp. Saving money. Leave for the city to study.

Hello. The son clicked his fingers. Refining his Asmara accent for her ears, he asked again: Whot – is – yoor – naame?

Saba noticed his thin lips, ravaged, she assumed, by biting. Perhaps from nerves, she thought. She was wondering whether to share with him tips on dealing with the first days in a camp. Yooo understaaaaand meee?

Tedros, basta cosi, the businessman said. Turning to Saba again, he asked: What's your name?

My name is Saba, she said.

Saba, Eyob said, I need someone to do chores – washing clothes, ironing. Can you do this?

Chirping reached Saba's ears. The birds sang loud, as if to make up for the lack of cockerels crowing. Nature has ways of rebalancing, of compensating for the absence of things.

She rose from her sleep and was soon dressed and on her way through the square to the east of the camp, on her way to start her first day as a domestic servant. She had after all inherited her mother's profession. She wanted to turn back inside the hut, wake her mother up and tell her the news that would perhaps mend some of what had broken between them.

In the early-morning light, other girls appeared. Some were going to the forest to fetch firewood. Others to the river to get water. And some to the aid centre to queue. Girls owned the square at this time of the day before dawn. Saba heard their giggles, their laughter, their greetings, the see-you-laters, the be-carefuls-of: the snakes in the forest, the strong current at the river that had claimed the lives of a few girls, and the men at the open toilet.

The sun dissolved the darkness. It was hot already.

When she arrived Tedros was standing next to a heap of dirty laundry by the wall of the main hut where the family of two slept. The second hut had been turned into a kitchen. A third made into storage for their boxes, stuffed with goods.

Tedros was wearing a T-shirt in the colours of the People's Liberation Front flag. The yellow Marxist star rested on his chest. His heart must beat to justice and equality, Saba thought, recalling Zahra's revolutionary slogans. She was about to collect the bundle of clothes and head to the river when Tedros stopped her. We have everything you need here, he said.

Saba followed Tedros with her eyes to the kitchen, from where he brought out a large yellow washing bucket, two metal pails, a small open furnace, charcoal, a metal pot, soap tablets, a stool, and a stiff impression pressed against his shorts.

You can use the water from the barrel, he said. But you must refill it after you finish.

He smelt of chocolate and powdered milk. He sat in front of her on his father's armchair as Saba set to work. She placed the water with a soap tablet to heat on the furnace, and separated the dirty laundry between whites and colours. After, she poured the hot soapy water into the bucket, and started with the white clothes. Steam rose from the bucket.

Saba heard snoring. She looked up at Tedros's long, thin face. His head slumped to the side. Saba was tempted to splash water on his face when she noticed a wet spot at the front of his shorts. That, she thought, I will have to wash later.

Tedros woke up when a group of parents arrived with crying babies. Please, sir.

Please give us what you can.

Our children are hungry.

Heal a mother's heart.

Tedros stormed inside the hut and slammed the door behind him. Saba wondered about his own mother, and why she wasn't here.

When Eyob emerged from his hut, he greeted Saba as he lowered himself into his armchair. Heat released fragrance from his neck. He opened a notebook, holding it open, but he didn't write a word. The blank pages flapped in the breeze. The nothingness of the camp has found its way to his lap already, Saba thought.

When Saba finished with her job, Tedros sauntered out of the hut holding cash. She couldn't recognize the currency. This is not birr, she said.

Birr! Tedros laughed and for the first time, Saba saw the gap between his front teeth. His face became rounder. And more appealing, she thought.

If you lived in the city you would know that the note in your hand is a pound note. We are in a different country.

He shook his head.

Saba looked at the creased note again. This is perfect, she thought. It was what she needed to save for her education in the city once refugees could leave the camp. Permission to travel, promised by the aid workers, couldn't come soon enough.

So you managed to find a job in a camp, said the Khwaja as he welcomed Saba. You are planning your departure already.

Who told you? Saba asked. One can't even keep thoughts and dreams secret in this place.

The Khwaja laughed. Here, let's go inside and study, he said.

Besides his yellow blanket, multi-coloured chair and jute sacks, he also had two books of poetry that he had promised to lend Saba once she could read English. His eyes bulged out when he put on his reading glasses. He jabbed his finger at the inequality article again. How can they have all this wealth and yet be so poorly versed in human matters?

The British graduate was on Saba's mind when she arrived at work the next morning. Saba greeted the businessman and headed to the kitchen hut to collect the laundry. It was locked. She tiptoed past Eyob to where Tedros was sleeping to get the keys. Good morning, Saba said, as Tedros stepped out.

What's good about life in this place? he asked.

He guffawed. A whiff of alcohol escaped his mouth.

With the keys in hand, Saba turned when she noticed Hagos walking towards them, balancing two jerrycans filled with water on a stick over his shoulders. He tripped over a stone and splashed water on Eyob.

Tedros rushed to his father's side. Papa, are you all right?

Eyob sat still, eyes fixed on Hagos. He said nothing.

Taking a handkerchief from his pocket, Tedros dried the water on his father's shirt. I am sorry, Saba said. I am so sorry.

Why doesn't he speak for himself? Tedros jumped to his feet, standing in front of Hagos.

Hagos didn't move. Some water still ran from the sides of the jerrycans suspended on the stick over his shoulders. The evening before, Saba had shared with her brother her plans for the future. Saba hoped Eyob would not get rid of her. Not now.

I am sorry, Sir Eyob, Saba said again. My brother didn't mean it.

But in her mind, she wasn't so sure. She wondered if her brother had deliberately set himself to get her fired and thwart the dream she had started to work towards, to leave this place.

Back in their hut, Saba lay in her blanket, wondering if she had lost her job. Usually, after she finished, Eyob would confirm another shift for the week ahead. This time, though, he said nothing. He just stared at Hagos again. And as his eyes settled on her brother, Saba noticed how the veins on Eyob's neck throbbed.

Lying on her blanket, Saba thought about Eyob and what it was about Hagos that had made the businessman's heart almost pulse out of his neck. Hagos stretched beside her and put his arm around her. Saba turned to face him. Hagos, did you do that on purpose? she asked.

Hagos looked away.

Did you want me to get fired?

Silence.

I mean, why else would you just come there without telling me?

Silence.

But how could you have told me?

Hagos tried to jerk away, but Saba held him back. I am sorry, she said.

In the evening, Saba, her hair washed and wrapped in a towel by Hagos, was sitting outside with her mother when the businessman came to their hut. Saba helped her mother to her feet. Welcome, Mr Eyob, the mother said. Your presence brightens our home.

You and everyone in your household is the source of this glow, he said.

May God bless you, the mother said.

Saba, I am not upset by what happened earlier today, Eyob said. In fact, it would be my pleasure if you want Hagos to help you at work.

Saba called on Hagos to come out. He squeezed himself between his sister and his mother. When his hand shook against her, Saba held it and caressed it with her thumb. Eyob greeted Hagos, then raised his head towards the sky, and as he looked back at Hagos again, Saba saw the glint in the businessman's eyes.

Silence.

Their mother coughed.

Ah, well, that's all. Actually, I am going for a walk. Hagos, the businessman said, I could do with some company. Would you like to join me?

I am sorry, Mr Eyob, the mother said. But my son would be no good. He doesn't talk.

Silence can make company even more interesting, Eyob smiled.

And as Hagos and Eyob entered the bustling square, where people asserted their existence with endless conversations, Saba felt as though Hagos was finally stepping outside his silent world.

Hagos was no longer invisible, she thought. People could see him now that he walked beside the businessman.

Hagos and the businessman walked daily. The businessman would come to pick up his new friend every evening. And the two would find their way to the outskirts of the camp. It is peaceful, Eyob told Saba and her mother one evening, as he waited for Hagos. He pointed to the wild hibiscus-filled hills bathing in the sunset. It suits us both.

But what suited them up in the hills? Saba wanted to ask. Was it the silence, the rugged landscape, the fresh air, the wild hibiscus or being away from people? Saba longed to hear Hagos's thoughts and feelings now that he had found a friend other than her.

Soapy water streamed from under the door.

Saba, tell your brother to hurry up, said the mother. How long does it take him to finish his bath?

I am not in a hurry, said the businessman.

A group of men and women crept up nearer. Their murmurs grew. Saba looked away from them. Hagos emerged in white T-shirt and shorts, smelling as if he'd bathed in Indian coconut oil.

The crowd parted. Eyob and Hagos set off to the outskirts of the camp where the sunset had settled into the curves of the hills adorned with wild flowers.

MEN ARE EASY TO READ

One evening, soon after Hagos and the businessman had set off for their walk, Saba took out a bucket to wash herself. Her mother was out having coffee with Samhiya's mother. Saba sat inside the bucket and closed her eyes, taking a deep breath. Peace in this place was only present in her imagination, so Saba imagined she was in a river, floating naked past trees, wilderness, villages, animals, life. She felt the rain on her body.

Peace, Saba mumbled, pressing her weight into the bucket, into a moment alone so blissful. The wind caressed back. It was making love to her, or so she felt as it blew through cracks in the door and walls and gaps in the thatched roof, stroking her wet skin from all directions, kissing her ears, the bone at her nape, the curves of her breasts. Saba wanted to possess. So she arched her back, revealing more of herself to the wind, directing this mysterious lover to where she liked to be touched and how.

With the elements at her behest, suddenly the door opened, her mother storming in past her, pulling her scarf over her face.

Saba dried her body and stood by the pole, as water dripped from her hair. She wrapped her arms around herself. A tremor of unsatisfied desire went through her. It took her a while before she managed to contain the fire under her wet skin. Instead of walking up to her mother, Saba sat on her blanket and asked her mother, in a low voice, what had happened.

Her mother didn't respond. Saba let out a long breath as if relieved by her mother's silence. But a familiar guilt resurfaced quickly when the mother hunched herself into a ball, making herself small. Seeing her mother in this position stirred Saba's soul, yet she couldn't move, she couldn't rush to her mother's side. She was sure that in the past she had known how to react to her mother's sadness.

Her head throbbed. She stood up, and was about to leave the hut, when the midwife arrived with Samhiya's mother. Saba lay back on the blanket and faced the wall, but she could still hear their conversation.

You should know by now, said Samhiya's mother. People talk. You have dodged bullets, you will survive sharp tongues. Come back, our coffee will get cold.

How can I sit there and listen to the things they are saying about my son? said the mother. You know what that man asked me, ah, why a wealthy educated businessman from the city is interested in a villager who is mute and cannot read or write?

Stop whimpering. At least they are not talking about her, for once, said the midwife, bringing a smile to Saba. And don't let crying be your first response. Can you not see it is good news?

What's good about people belittling my son?

Saba smiled when her mother talked back at the midwife, an elation that didn't last when the midwife said: Think for yourself and try to understand why Eyob is doing it. I expected you to realize this, but let me explain.

You don't need to explain, said the mother. That man told me my son is... I can't even say it.

God forgive us, said the midwife. Don't even say it. We don't have these things in our culture. Eyob is a man of God. He was married and he has a son. How can he do that if he goes with boys, ah? But people in this camp are jealous of your son and you.

The midwife laughed. Listen to this carefully. Men, my dear, are easy to read. The businessman is in love with Saba and he is waiting for her to become a woman.

That makes sense, Saba heard Samhiya's mother say. In our country, men used to buy jewellery to make a girl love them. But we are in a camp, and all we have left is each other to use to get what we want.

Saba lifted the scarf off her face and glared at the wall. The women talked about her as if she wasn't in the hut. As if she couldn't hear. Yet, she was the centre of their attention. And for that they had to make her invisible in their eyes.

Saba turned her attention back to the women. The midwife's words seemed to placate Saba's mother. But then her tone sounded heavy, as if all sorrows passed through her throat at the same time as her words when she lamented that her daughter would marry before her older brother.

Hagos was in Saba's mind later that evening as she watched her brother return from his evening stroll with the businessman. Eyob stood on the other side of the square, close to the aid centre. Hagos stopped and turned to look back at the businessman. He waved and continued on his way home, towards Saba.

Until now, before overhearing that conversation between the women earlier, Saba had imagined other reasons for Eyob's befriending of Hagos. She knew people liked to talk and were in need of good listeners, but it was also clear that the businessman appreciated silence. Hagos could provide Eyob with both: listen whenever he wanted to talk and be quiet whenever he preferred silence, without having to be asked.

This advantage people had over Hagos wasn't new. Saba remembered the times back home when she overheard her cousin telling Hagos about her love affairs. Without a voice, Hagos was a safe with keys that no one would ever find. Saba knew this very well, and felt total freedom in his presence. She'd even masturbate knowing that even if he woke up, he couldn't tell anyone. Her desires and secrets were safe in Hagos's chest.

Hagos hugged Saba. She smelt Eyob's cologne on his skin and that confirmed in her mind how close the businessman was getting to Hagos in order to get to her. Yes, she loved her brother but she never meant for that love to carry another man to her on its wave.

Hagos took off his shirt and lay in his blanket, facing the wall. Saba sat next to him. Sweat rolled down his back. Saba steadied her hand as she wiped perspiration off his skin. She imagined some time from now when Eyob would succeed and her brother would be left behind, dying a virgin as the men at Azyeb's bar had predicted.

THE PROSTITUTE

Saba collected the laundry to take to the river while Hagos cooked. This division of labour suited them both. Saba craved the outside and the silence away from the camp, while Hagos preferred home life.

At the river, Saba sat far away from the crowd of people but when she heard whimpering she realized she wasn't alone. A shaven-headed young girl sat nearby, arms wrapped around her ankles, chin on her knees, staring out at the water.

Saba walked up and sat next to her. Is everything all right? she asked.

The girl did not respond. Saba sat close, rubbing her back, and asked again what was wrong. Eventually the girl raised her head, weeping freely now. Saba hugged her close and gently coaxed the story out of her. The young girl had been beaten by her parents earlier that day when they found out she worked for a prostitute. The midwife told my father, the girl said. But I didn't know she was sharmota. I went to ask her for a job when I saw her unload nice furniture when she arrived in the camp.

Saba remembered the woman who arrived from the city the same night as Eyob and Tedros.

Nasnet is generous, full of joy and has a good heart, the girl said in a whisper, thanking Saba for talking to her.

It was a scorching afternoon and the place was almost deserted when Saba arrived at Nasnet's hut. She could do with some laughter, Saba decided as she knocked. The door creaked open. A woman of average height with long curly hair and a silky nightgown shuffled out.

Yes? asked Nasnet, rubbing her face, yawning.

You look tired, Saba said. Maybe I should leave you alone and come back later.

Come back, why? Nasnet asked.

I know your help left and I thought you might need a new one.

Thank you but no. I need to sleep now. Nasnet shut the door.

Saba knocked again. Nasnet opened, and this time hissed: Don't you know what they are all saying about me? I am a prostitute. I am diseased.

Do you need a helper or not?

Nasnet stared at Saba. Did you see what happened to that poor girl? Did you see how badly she was beaten because she worked for me?

I can start tomorrow morning, said Saba.

Nasnet looked at Saba but said nothing.

Can I start tomorrow? Please.

When Saba arrived at Nasnet's the next morning, her new employer emerged with her hair in pink rollers and a mountain of laundry in her arms. It was a busy night, Nasnet said, winking. Good business for me means good pay for you.

I need to advertise your services then, Saba said.

Nasnet laughed. Come, sweetheart, let's go to my kitchen, she said, kicking the door of an adjacent hut open with her foot.

Saba wondered how Nasnet had managed to get two huts for herself. She decided not to ask. Dropping the pile of clothes next to a bucket placed between an open furnace and a box with pots and knives, Nasnet turned and asked Saba to sit. This is a nice leather stool, she said. I'll leave you to it now. But I'll come and join you when I finish with my hair. We can talk then.

Saba nodded, smiling. But when she held the bedcovers in her hands, about to dip them into the bucket, she froze. She pushed her stool back and leaned against the wall. As she shut her eyes to bring herself back to the task at hand, she saw Nasnet rolling on the sheet, arms reaching over her. Nasnet was trapped, unable to breathe under the weight of a man. Different men. Yet, Saba couldn't reconcile the Nasnet she had seen and talked to with the image in her mind.

Saba opened her eyes and plunged her hands into the bucket. She expected the bedcovers to be soaked in men's sweat, their release. But there was no trace of their presence in the clothes she was washing, only a tinge of floral-scented perfume. There was no sign either of Nasnet's nervousness on the sheets or of perspiration on her clothes. Saba wondered if only true love would bring out a lasting aroma.

Nasnet moved back and forth between her hut and the kitchen. Every time she saw Nasnet, Saba scrutinized her face, as if to unearth the pain, the unhappiness, that a sex worker must feel. She couldn't imagine that Nasnet liked her job.

But Nasnet's laughter infected Saba. She couldn't remember laughing as much as when she was around her new boss – it was as if pleasure was what everyone sought and obtained in Nasnet's presence. The next shift couldn't come soon enough.

Her mother, though, found out about Saba's new job soon after.

Late one morning, after she had arrived home from Eyob's, Saba went straight in to lie on her blanket without acknowledging the midwife and the two other women sitting with her. Saba wanted to have a little nap before heading out to Nasnet.

What have I done to deserve this? Saba heard her mother's complaint, but she snored, pretending to be sleeping.

And what will Mr Eyob say if he found out your daughter is working for a sex worker now? the midwife asked. He will abandon her. She doesn't need the money. Eyob has plenty of it. She did it to spite you. Your dream is over before it started.

Why, what have I done to you?

Saba? Your mother is talking to you, get up and listen.

Saba could barely see the midwife's green eyes through the smoke twisting off the incense burner. The hut was sweltering. Saba's chest tightened.

Do you know how humiliating it is for a man to see someone he wants to marry working for a prostitute? Is that what you want to be too, a whore?

The midwife's words snatched Saba out of her lethargy. She was up on her feet: No. I want to be a doctor. I want to make my own money, save my own money so I can go to school somewhere else. Now, I need to sleep.

Saba lifted her blanket off the floor, lay on the bare ground and spread the cover over herself, though she could still hear the women discussing the problem of Saba, talking at the same time, interrupting each other, yelling to make their point heard.

They complained about her stubbornness, her selfishness, her lack of sensitivity, complaints she had always ignored as if they were spoken in a foreign language. Saba wondered if it was possible for all these women to be wrong about her.

She is not young any more, the midwife said. When we were her age, we cared for our families and some of us even bore children. Saba's only concern is herself. When was the last time I slept and ate without interruption? I am awake most nights going from one hut to another, attending pregnant women, caring for the sick. In our culture, for girls, the pain and feelings of others come first. But I promise you, I will expel your daughter's demons. If she keeps on this path, you will die before your time. Look at you.

Saba threw off her blanket and looked at her mother. Her frazzled grey hair strayed from under her scarf. Her sharp bones framed her dress like a clothes hanger. And according to the midwife it wasn't due to life in the camp or the pain of exile. It was because of Saba. Saba was killing her mother.

The midwife opened a bag and prayed as she poured berbere on the incense burner. The embers sparked and sizzled. Smoke rose everywhere. It formed a barrier between Saba and the women inside the hut, women who sought to make her better. Burn her unfeminine traits on this fire, as if this were chaff clinging to her skin.

Mother, said Saba. I am sorry I am not the kind of daughter you always wanted to have. I never will be.

Saba left to go back to work. When she stood in front of Nasnet, her boss said, You smell as if you have been cooked in chilli. What happened?

Silence.

Have they found out you are working for me?

Silence.

They did, didn't they?

Saba sat in front of the bucket.

No, you are not working today, said Nasnet. Here, come inside and take a shower.

Saba didn't move.

Come, said Nasnet. Please.

Saba gave her hand to the woman, who led her inside the hut where only men had been. Saba cast her eyes around. To the left of the door, there was a blue plastic chair lined up against the wall. Right next to it, under the window, stood a small table. Covered in colourful fabric, it was arranged with a set of china cups and silk flowers in a blue plastic vase. Further, next to the tape recorder on top of an upside-down sardine box, there was a slim wardrobe, and next to that the bed. For Saba, a bed had up to now been a place to sleep, study and dream. Here, it had a different purpose altogether. She looked away.

Come on, get ready, Nasnet said, setting off to prepare the bath. She rolled up a jute rug and lined it up against one side of the hut, and drew out a large washing bucket from under her bed. Placing it by the pole, Nasnet then strode out of the hut. Saba's eyes darted around the hut again. The amount of furniture made the hut smaller, but the decoration and colour reminded her of when she was in her own room back home.

Nasnet returned with scented soap, shampoo and a pail with water which she placed next to the washing bucket. She gasped. Pressing a hand to her chest, Nasnet asked, My God, Saba, what happened to your thighs?

Nothing. Saba lowered herself into the bucket.

I'm sorry, Nasnet said, hugging Saba close.

Saba sank into her friend's embrace, closing her eyes. I'm fine now. But they wanted to silence me head to toe. Shut my mouth and cut off the lips of my vagina. But I am still talking.

Nasnet's tears fell. I am sorry, she said to Saba. Maybe I shouldn't cry but I can't help it.

Saba smiled. Come on now then, give me a bath.

Sometimes you are like a man, so forcibly charming, Nasnet blurted out.

Saba didn't deny the comparison. That's what the midwife has told me since I was a little girl. She thinks it is an insult.

They laughed again before Nasnet said, Come darling, let me wash you. I need to get ready for work.

Do you hate the midwife? Saba asked.

Why would I? Nasnet said, now washing the soap out of Saba's hair.

She gave away your secret, Saba said.

White froth rolled down her chest.

I didn't choose for my job to be a secret, Nasnet said. It's ironic, though. Society makes it so and then they try to oust you and ostracize you for the secret they have demanded and imposed in the first place.

Saba's eyes met Nasnet's. What, Nasnet said, you didn't expect a prostitute to talk like this?

Saba smiled.

I love those dimples, Nasnet said, pinching Saba's cheek.

After cleaning Saba's back, Nasnet passed the soap to Saba. Here, you do the rest, she said, sitting on her bed.

Did you do that because of your job? Saba asked Nasnet, pointing to the three patterned lines made of small cone shapes tattooed across Nasnet's neck.

No, I did this when I was seven. I saw the daughter of a rich landowner wearing a beautiful necklace, and asked my mother if I could have one too. My mother couldn't afford it, but a friend of hers suggested a tattoo on my neck instead. For days, I refused to accept my mother's proposal. I thought she didn't love me if she wouldn't even buy me a simple necklace. But my mother's friend told me that the Queen of Sheba had a tattoo even though she could buy anything she wanted, so

I finally accepted. Besides, I told myself then, a tattoo necklace would never break or get lost.

Nasnet paused and, craning her head backwards, she asked: Do you like it?

Saba nodded: It makes you look special. It goes well with the clothes you have.

Both laughed. Nasnet more so. Saba watched her laughter again, as if hoping to learn from it, and embrace it.

Saba stood, her feet still in the water, her shadow on the wall of Nasnet's hut rising with her, the reflection of her nipples shifting with the flickering of the oil lamp. And when she was about to leave Nasnet's hut, smelling of coconut cream, Nasnet hugged her. With their cheeks still touching, Saba whispered a thank you.

Saba, Nasnet said. You know this is a camp. People are generous with what they have in the hope they will get something they don't. So if you want to borrow some privacy, I can lend you my hut. You can come any time.

Saba looked at the bed with the thick mattress and blue cover. She imagined the men in this bed, imagined Nasnet under them. Nasnet turned Saba's head away. As if she could read her eyes, Nasnet said: Luckily, I don't break easily. And I feel you are someone who doesn't either.

But Saba returned home absent-minded. The happiness she experienced around Nasnet brought anxiety to her. Her relationship with the sex worker felt like a deliberate rebellion against her mother. In truth, though, Saba knew that everything she loved, everything she did naturally, would meet with disapproval. Saba's instincts were the cause of her mother's anguish. My existence itself is a crime, Saba thought, back in her hut. She sat on her blanket and closed her eyes.

The door was flung open. Zahra came in. Saba stirred. Can you not knock?

I'm sorry I surprised you.

What do you want? Saba asked. I need some sleep.

We ran out of salt and oil and I thought I could cook our lentils here and share them between us. But maybe you want me to go?

Saba shrugged.

Are you all right, Saba?

Yes.

Saba? What's going on?

It's the mother, said Saba. I wish she was more like yours.

How do you know my mother would have been different? asked Zahra.

She is a fighter, said Saba.

All women are fighters, said Zahra. It is just that we fight different wars. My mother carrying a gun doesn't make her stronger than your mother, who's been fighting for you since your father left.

Is that what your grandmother said?

I am capable of thinking for myself, Saba. Anyway, I came to cook with you. That's all. And by the way, you should stop calling your mother The Mother.

As she turned, about to leave, Zahra said, I am going now, but maybe by the time we see each other again, you will have remembered your mother's name.

THE MOTHER'S NAME

M^{ehret.}

SHARING

One evening, Saba and Hagos were sitting outside their hut when Samhiya stopped by. I just want to say good evening to the beautiful brother and sister, said Samhiya.

Saba felt Hagos squeeze her hand tightly as his eyes followed Samhiya's swinging hips. Saba felt his warmth surge through her arm.

Soon after, the judge and the committee of elders arrived in the square. They stood between the mosque and the spot where the priest held his daily prayers. Tradition is the third religion in the camp, Saba thought, as the judge mounted a chair and began preaching to the residents through his megaphone.

He squinted as he looked across the crowd, even though the sun had already sunk behind the hill. Either plenty of time has passed since we came here, or some age quicker than others, Saba thought, as she inspected her own body for signs of change. The wounds Saba had amassed over the time she had been in the camp had healed but left permanent reminders of a clock ticking, like the black patches on her left forearm and both knees.

Oil lamps flickered. A haze of yellow-orange light stretched across the square. Faces like flowers bloomed in the evening.

I am going to the toilet, Saba said to her brother.

Hagos stood up and put on his shoes. Holding hands, the brother and sister walked past the judge as he concluded his lecture with a message:

The world has forgotten about us, but we could not have lasted in this place without understanding that our existence is dependent on us sharing with each other.

Saba wrapped an arm around Hagos and tickled his waist with her long nails.

Saba dipped her hands into the bucket, scrubbing the dirt out of the father and son's shirts, as gently as she did to her own skin. The life of clothes had to be extended for as long as possible. The morning sun followed its path in the sky, dispersing heat in its wake. Eyob left his hut barefoot, tucking in his shirt, buttons still undone. Greying hair clustered on his chest. He greeted passers-by and waved at those standing in the distance.

The businessman is smiling at us, some of the children said, applauding, only to flee when Eyob's whistling drew Tedros out of the hut.

I thought you said whistling was satanic, eh Papa? he laughed.

Parents are contradictory, Eyob said, smiling at his son.

Well, I am happy to see you in a good mood, Tedros said. But what happened to you? You look like a refugee yourself now.

Tedros laughed and sat next to his father. He clicked his fingers. Saba, tea.

Saba, though, didn't respond to her name wrapped in Tedros's morning breath. Eyob took the pot that Saba had prepared off the furnace and poured tea for his son.

The father and son talked as if Saba wasn't there.

My younger self is finding a new life in a refugee camp, said the businessman. It is never too late to be who you truly are. Hagos taught me that.

Saba stopped and pulled her hands out of the bucket. She looked up. Her face met the sun, yet Eyob's words burnt her inside with the thought that her brother, in Eyob's eyes, was a source of wisdom, of change, and not a recipient of pity or sympathy.

Tedros's call woke her from her reverie. No dreaming here, he said.

Saba resumed the washing, her ears opened to the father and son's conversation.

Eyob and Tedros reminisced about the past. About the time a five-year-old Tedros clung to their maid's breasts and had to be pulled away. They laughed. My aunt always said you should have married her, said Tedros.

Yes, my dear sister thought of every woman I met as a suitable wife for me.

She wanted you to be happy, Father.

Why do people assume you only find happiness when you are married? Eyob said, raising his voice.

Like my aunt said, Father, you are handsome, well-educated, wealthy. Any beautiful woman would fall at your feet, said Tedros.

Yet, a beautiful woman left me.

Tedros didn't respond.

I am sorry to remind you of your mother, Eyob said.

I've lived a happy life without her, his son replied.

Tedros, please. I want you to understand that your mother had reasons for leaving me.

And leaving her two-year-old child too?

Regardless of what your mother did or didn't do, she alone is responsible for her actions, not all women.

So why didn't you marry then, after she left?

Eyob didn't answer. He pressed his palms onto the arms of his chair and pushed himself up. He entered the hut and shut the door. Saba sat straight, soapy water dripped from her hands. Tedros's eyes rested on her naked feet. They travelled up her legs, free from her dress that had slid above her knees to expose new bruises, old gashes and purple thighs. He went into the kitchen.

Saba hung the clothes on a line and as she looked up the hill, she saw Jamal digging two long poles into the ground. A large white sheet was drying on a clothesline in front of his hut. His flat cap fell as he straightened his back and wiped his forehead.

THE RAZOR

Weeks after Saba returned from the hospital having had treatment for her burns, the midwife entered her room holding a razor, the mother behind her. Saba had yet to understand why the midwife had become obsessed with her vagina, but the woman's persistence about executing this rite, about ridding Saba of a piece she carried on her body unaware, made her wonder if it was for her own good, as important as washing the dirt off her skin, as necessary as amputating an infected limb. But the thing the midwife aimed her razor at as her mother restrained her was the very thing Saba touched to pleasure herself. So that afternoon, Saba called for Hagos as she fought to release herself from her mother's grip. Hagos. Help me. Hagos?

No answer.

Saba pushed her mother out of the way. The midwife, though, blocked the door with her body. Do you want to be a prostitute? she said to Saba, fury in her eyes. Please sit down. We are doing it for your own good.

WOMEN DYING LIKE MEN

A meeting was called by the aid workers. The Englishman and his assistant stood on a couple of chairs placed next to each other. Saba sweated. She wondered why the aid coordinator liked to have his meetings when the sun was at its strongest.

Saba inspected the Englishman's tanned face as the athlete, standing ahead of her, joked to the light-skinned assistant that soon he would look the more English of the two.

Hopefully we will be back home before we see such a miracle, said the praise poet.

The crowd laughed, and a few shouts of Amen rang out. Saba was hugged from behind. She turned her head to find Zahra's chin resting on her shoulder. I love you, said the fighter's daughter.

Saba caressed Zahra's cheeks.

Do you want to come to our hut tonight to read my mother's pamphlets? Zahra asked.

Yes, Saba said. If your grandmother will let me touch them.

Zahra laughed. She's just worried they will be damaged.

Let's listen, said Saba. The Englishman is talking.

We have good news to share with you, said the Englishman via his interpreter, after paying tribute to the elders for their patience and for managing to maintain peace in the refugee camp. I am happy to report that our request for a large storage building has been accepted. We will soon have storage large enough to stock better food and extra blankets. God willing.

Applause broke out. Promises are enough when action is meaningless, Saba thought, as the aid workers dismounted from the chairs and were replaced by the singer and her nephew with the double-headed drum.

The singer sang about her gratefulness for not being forgotten by the world.

People like us fear invisibility, Saba said to Zahra. Just look how we shout when we could whisper, and laugh when smiles are enough.

Yeeeess. Zahra's scream made Saba laugh.

Our beautiful world is closer than we thought, the singer continued, improvising a song.

A dancing throng formed a circle around the singer.

Let's go, Zahra said.

Wait, Saba said, weaving her way through the crowd until she found the aid coordinator's assistant. She asked about the school. The assistant cupped a hand behind his ear. Saba raised her voice. Did you also get permission to build our school? she asked. Is it going to be built at the same time as the new aid centre?

The assistant wagged his finger at her. Not now, he said. Look around, everyone is happy.

Zahra grabbed Saba by the hand and pulled her away.

The two girls sat by Saba's hut. Saba, be patient, Zahra said. First things first, how can hungry people study? How can you lift a pen if you can't even lift your arm?

In the same way we lift our arms to eat, said Saba.

Why? Why do you say that? I know this will upset you, Saba. But I really think there must always be room for hunger in our stomachs, in our hearts, our minds, our souls. It is that hunger that will lead us to become fighters for our freedom, so we can determine our own future.

But have you thought about what will happen afterwards? Saba asked.

What do you mean?

Well, if we all become fighters who will rebuild our destroyed homes after independence? Who will build our schools, our clinics, bridges, roads? Who will treat the ill and educate children?

The dancing circle grew wider, almost reaching Saba's hut. Saba stood up. I'm going, she said.

Wait for me, said Zahra. I am coming with you.

The two friends held hands and made their way to the field assigned for the promised school. As Saba sat on the rock, Zahra stood next to her.

I saw my mother in my sleep again last night, carrying another wound, Zahra said. She joined Saba on the rock, her bony elbow grazing Saba's rib. Sometimes I am afraid that my mother is dead. And if she is dead, I need to go and replace her.

Saba said nothing, her chest heaved. Zahra leaned forward. A bird landed on the grass opposite, and chirped. Saba picked up a stone and threw it. The bird flew away with her false hope.

We can't let men do the fighting for us, said Zahra. That's what my mother says in her tape. We can't wait for our freedom. We have to fight for it. We must be ready to die like men for our dreams. They are our dreams too.

Zahra stood up and started plucking out the long grass with her bare hands. Come on. Let's at least start clearing this site. I might be leaving soon, but you must stay in the camp. You are right, we can't all be fighters.

Then Zahra extended her arms towards Saba. Rough hands – hands that had scrubbed clothes at the river banks, carried jerrycans from the river, collected firewood in the bush – touched. Zahra helped Saba to her feet.

They both bent down, their shoulders touching the yellow dry grass, their hands at the roots, pulling them out, clearing the field to make it ready for the school.

Saba arrived at the businessman's hut for a new shift later than usual. She had spent the night with Zahra and her grandmother listening to one of the fighter's tapes full of songs, tales from the front, and reading some of the pamphlets the mother sent from the front to her daughter.

It was as if she had drunk from the fighter's words of determination. I will never marry, Saba vowed to herself when Eyob stood up to wave at the midwife walking in the distance. I will never marry anyone.

Saba was about to take her chair and bucket full of clothes away from the businessman's view when she remembered what Zahra's grandmother had told her the evening before. Be resolute inside yourself and strong but don't change your behaviour towards that man, the grandmother said to Saba. Don't give him or anyone else the pleasure of knowing that they changed you.

Eyob tilted his head to the side and called his son.

Tedros yawned. Alcohol saturated the air and Saba held her breath, hoping it would pass. Here, Tedros, sit, his father said. And drink your tea. I need to talk to you.

It's hard to hear you, Father, if she keeps making noise with that washing of hers.

Tedros gulped down the last drops of his tea and told Saba to show some respect to his father and wash quietly, like a girl. Maybe we should have hired Hagos instead, he said, snorting.

Saba continued with her work.

Listen, Tedros. I know I told you I will find a way back to the city. But I want us to stay here and open the shop we always wanted.

A shop? Saba raised her head. Her anger dissipated.

And you still think these refugees have money to spend, Father? Tedros laughed.

I'm sure many do, said Eyob. These people had jobs back home, just like me.

There's another reason why you want to stay in the camp, said Tedros. But it doesn't matter, whatever makes you happy. I'm leaving the day they allow us to leave.

The businessman left for the aid centre, saying he was going to ask for a permit to open a shop.

The aid coordinator agreed to write to the authorities in the city, but weeks passed and nothing happened. When Saba asked the Khwaja, during an English lesson, why the businessman and all those other entrepreneurs evicted from the city didn't open businesses, like Azyeb and Nasnet had done, the Khwaja remarked that fear of the unknown was what was holding many back. Remember, Saba, they were uprooted from the city by the authorities early one morning as they were readying themselves to go to work, to open their shops, to drive their taxis, to sell groceries in the market. The new life they had invested in ended the moment armed soldiers knocked on their doors at dawn. They are afraid. But I am sure it will pass. First we root our sensibility in the camp, and with each seed sown a bit of that fear is stripped off.

THE SHOP

Saba was queuing for the weekly ration one afternoon when the businessman arrived in the square with a group of men carrying thatch and wood.

A crowd assembled.

Here, he said to the men, pointing at a spot where he wanted his shop to be built, opposite Saba's hut and to the left of the aid centre.

Once the aid coordinator and his assistant appeared in front of him, Eyob shook the Englishman's hand and turned to his assistant and translator. Please tell your boss that when I am excited I prefer to speak my own language. I am now ready to open my shop and start the path to self-reliance for us all.

The aid coordinator looked at Eyob with his usual calm. When he spoke, though, Saba detected irritation in his voice: But, Mr Eyob, he said through his translator, you need a permit first. These are the rules.

We have waited long enough, said Eyob. Waiting for school, clothes, better food since the first day here. And there is no need to wait for things we can do ourselves.

I understand, the aid coordinator said. But you must be aware of the sheer volume of similar requests authorities in the city have to deal with. There are hundreds of refugee camps around the country.

That's why it is best we take matters into our own hands, said Eyob. That way, we will alleviate the burden on you and the donors in the long term. And let me tell you something I learnt about capitalism in your economy.

The translator shook his head. Don't, he said to Eyob in Tigrinya. This man is a socialist. I can't translate this.

I will do it, said Eyob. Addressing the Englishman directly in English that Saba understood in parts, the businessman said, You see, this is going to be a simple shop, but we must start somewhere. Dignity and self-worth are doubly important in shoring up our spirits and so forth. Thereafter, we hope our people will be in a position to open their own businesses. As your Adam Smith said: The real tragedy of the poor is the poverty of their aspirations.

When the Khwaja translated Eyob's words to those around him, a rapturous applause erupted. He can have his three huts as long as he gives us words like this, said Samhiya, to everyone's laughter.

Before long, Eyob had built a thatched kiosk. Saba's eyes darted around its interior. Light flickered through the windows. Since there were no shelves, boxes were lined up against the wall on three sides, with representative samples placed on top of each: green coffee beans, sugar, frankincense, cigarettes, heart-shaped lollipops, berbere and shoro. Next to the incense deposited in straw baskets were rectangular tin containers filled with halva.

The excitement that followed the opening of the shop faded after a few weeks. Saba, who saved every penny she earned, didn't buy anything, but instead took a journey down the memory lanes evoked by the shop's products, back to her homeland, just as many others did.

One evening, Saba sat outside her hut, resting her head on Hagos's shoulder as he massaged their mother's hands. People were seated all over the square in groups. Sounds of laughter echoed around her. Saba turned to look at the shop at the moment when an eagle landed on its roof and began to tear at the thatch with its beak. Eyob hurried out of his shop and threw a stone at the large black bird. Soon after, he came to Saba's to pick up Hagos, holding two packages. He handed the halva to Hagos and gave the pack of coffee to Saba and her mother, saying it was for both of them. When Saba told the businessman that she didn't drink coffee, her mother poked her in the ribs with her elbow. Thank you and may God bless you, their mother said to Eyob.

Weeks passed and still few people bought anything at the shop. Eyob tried to adapt his business model by selling single items: one cigarette at a time, a handful of coffee beans, a few spoonfuls of shoro and berbere. The change in strategy, though, still didn't lead to a boost in revenue.

One morning, father and son discussed the shop as Saba washed their laundry. I shouldn't be called a businessman any more, Eyob said. Opening this shop was a mistake.

I told you so, said Tedros. He smirked as he shook his head.

People are holding on to their money so they can use it for their transport back home once the war ends, said Eyob. And when I asked the aid coordinator if they could provide people with loans to open businesses and work for themselves, he told me they were just an aid relief organization and had no loans to authorize.

But why don't you give loans yourself?

The father and son turned their heads to look at Saba.

What?

No, let her speak, Tedros.

My grandmother used to lend money to people. She said new businesses stimulate old ones.

I did that too, said Eyob, but they could put their own homes, farms, cars and even bicycles as collateral against borrowing. How can anyone here guarantee my money, if even the huts they live in belong to the government of this country? This is not viable.

Eyob left for his shop with his breakfast untouched.

This camp is full of delusional people, Tedros said, swaggering to the kitchen hut.

As Saba arched her back, sweat rolling down from her forehead, she spotted the shop's keys on the chair.

When Saba arrived at the shop with his keys, Eyob was standing with arms folded, staring at the long queue outside the aid centre that meandered across the square and reached the shop. Eyob shook his head. What a waste, he said as he turned his back to the queue brimming with potential customers and took the keys from Saba.

Saba looked at the aid centre, the place from which she and her family got their free food. The place that kept them alive. But there is more to life, she thought, turning to the shop, and the man who gave her work and the chance to dream of a future.

Here, what do you think of this? Nasnet asked Saba, twirling around to show off her yellow dress. My client today is one of the aid workers. Maybe he will help me get out of this camp.

Please don't leave, said Saba.

You only say that because you are scared of losing your job, said Nasnet. Perhaps you can take my place.

Now that will only make the midwife happy, said Saba. And make her prophecy come true.

Nasnet laughed and sat on the bed next to Saba.

Can I ask you a question?

Yes, said Nasnet, putting on her earrings.

Has my brother ever come to see you?

Nasnet turned and raised her brows. Saba, I am like my doctor back home. I never reveal any information about my clients, she said. Now come and help me choose shoes to go with this dress.

MEAT

The ground around Saba's hut shook. Thinking new refugees had arrived, she hurried to watch from her door as children scampered off in different directions, running from the herd of cows and sheep stamping their way into the square. Her mother came out too and stood next to Saba. Through the thick cloud of dust Saba noticed a man, a woman and a young girl rushing around the edges of the herd on their donkeys.

The square was taken over by animals. A bull stared back at Saba, green saliva drooling from his grass-filled mouth. How long had it been since she had seen a cow, a sheep, heard the braying of a donkey?

Saba walked closer to the animals. A goat rubbed its horn against her leg, a cockerel with a leash around its leg tried to pick at her foot. A wave of animal odour washed over the square and she breathed it all in.

Next to the woman, who had taken a kitten out of a basket and held it in the palms of her hands to show to the children around her, Saba observed a girl in a shin-length red dress, with plaited hair and a half-crescent nose ring. Saba tried to imagine what this girl's life must be like, moving from one place to another, with this huge herd of animals. Her home the sum of fragments of different places. The young traveller went around her animals, as though they were her best friends, stroking and quieting them.

As her attention returned to the animals in front of her, Saba realized the potential for business if the nomads stayed. Seized by that impulsive thought, she ran to Eyob's hut in the east of the camp. Saba was breathless on her arrival.

Mr Eyob.

Please. What can I do for you?

Saba hesitated to say what she was thinking, but when she heard the bray of the donkey, the lowing of the cows, she wanted these animals to stay in the camp, not only to make business, but also to make life more colourful and more real. Besides, she craved the shoro with beef that Hagos had cooked for her back home.

Saba talked quickly: Did you hear? Nomads and their herd just arrived at our camp. There is a man here with animals and I wanted to let you know. Just think of the opportunity, of selling milk, eggs, butter for ga'at and meat.

Saba paused and beamed as she continued: We could finally have shoro with beef.

Eyob sprang to his feet and sped ahead of her. Saba had never seen him walk this fast. She ran to keep up. When they arrived back in the square, Eyob told her to wait for him outside her hut. She stood next to her mother, watching him as he tiptoed around the animals and stepped over the dung with flies buzzing on top of it. The businessman embraced the stranger as if he were a long-lost relation.

Moments later, Saba saw Eyob, her mother and the nomad man, who had a long stick and a dishevelled vest over his jellabiya, walking towards her. Eyob asked Saba's mother if he could use her hut for a quick meeting. His own hut was too far for a man who had been travelling for days on foot.

Our honour, Saba's mother said, asking Saba to go inside and clean the hut.

No need, the businessman said. But tea would be most appreciated.

The nomad stretched his hand towards Saba's mother and said, Let me introduce myself. My name is Hajj Ali.

The way he spoke Arabic reminded Saba of Tahir, their lorry driver.

The entire camp has turned out to welcome you, Saba's mother said to Hajj Ali. We don't get visitors here.

We were led here by our animals, said Hajj Ali. And yes, sometimes they take us to the forgotten people.

Inside the hut, as the businessman and Hajj Ali sat on stools, Saba lit the open furnace to boil tea.

I would like to discuss with you an important matter, the businessman said. I know from my brief stay in the city that the people of this country never leave a request unheard.

Hajj Ali smiled. True, he said. I'm happy to oblige.

As Saba closed the door, she noticed heads jostling for a view through the window. She didn't pull down the straw curtain. She knew of the necessity of leaving a window open upon a girl's dealings with men.

I am sorry you had to open your home to a stranger without notice, the nomad said to Saba.

We are the strangers in your country, Saba said, reverting to the Arabic she learnt from her trader grandmother.

Masha Allah, said Hajj Ali, nodding. To some, wisdom arrives without roaming from one place to another.

The nomad sat on a stool next to the businessman. He placed his sword against his leg and his stick on the floor. Is she your daughter? he asked Eyob.

Saba looked at Eyob. Her eyes lingered on his face, as if hoping he would say, No, but Saba is like my daughter. But the businessman didn't respond. Moments passed before his answer came: No, she works for me.

You are a lucky man, the nomad said.

Saba tried not to think about Eyob, about what the midwife had said, because thinking about him threatened to centre her life around a man. She wanted to be more than that. She turned her attention back to the conversation at hand.

If I may start, Eyob said.

Please go ahead, said the nomad.

The water boiled. Saba added the tea leaves.

Hajj Ali, said Eyob, everyone in this camp is tired of powdered milk and tinned rations. Everyone longs for fresh food. No one forgets those who feed them as they would like to eat themselves.

Saba's eyes rested on Hajj Ali's broad forehead, his bulging eyes. His bony face appeared like a chiselled rock. He was shaped by the elements he encountered on his journey, she thought. Humans, like the earth, are vulnerable to wind and water, to nature. How much had she herself changed since living in the camp?

The tea was ready. But, fearing the businessman would ask her to leave once it was served, Saba kept it on the fire. She listened on as Eyob continued his efforts to persuade the nomad to stay.

The food we get from the aid centre just keeps us alive, said the businessman. But we need more than that. We need business to get our lives back.

The nomad didn't say anything. Just as his body and face survived the elements in their most hostile form on his travels, he stood firm against Eyob's attempt to appeal to his emotions.

I hope you will think of this from the goodness in your heart, said Eyob. Business that combines kindness is the most profitable.

But how will my presence help business? Hajj Ali asked.

I am confident our businesses will complement each other, the businessman said. When people buy meat from you, they will buy oil, onions and tomatoes from me. Think of the profit you could make.

Hajj Ali wiped saliva from the corners of his mouth with his hands. Eyob asked Saba if the tea was ready.

Allow the girl to take her time, said the nomad. We like our tea as strong as our women. He smiled, turning to Saba: How old are you?

I don't know when I was born, Saba replied.

My mother always told me, the nomad said, that a woman who doesn't care about age is a woman who keeps her youth in her heart.

Saba poured tea for the men. Hajj Ali slurped and muttered thanks to God. He asked for more sugar. As Saba brought the extra sugar from a box behind the door, she felt his eyes on her back, and when she turned, his attention focused on her legs.

God bless you, he said, as he sipped on the tea sweetened to his liking.

Turning to Eyob, he asked: But why is the shop closed at this time of the day?

People are not spending because they think they will leave, but it doesn't look like the war back home will end anytime soon. Maybe the best thing to make that money flow again is to bring more business into the camp rather than less.

I presume this money you are talking about is your own currency, said the nomad. I don't plan to go to a war zone.

I can exchange our country's money for your currency, the businessman said.

Anyway, forgive us, but we are nomads. I am not sure we can stay, Hajj Ali said as he fixed his turban, taking in the muscles of Saba's calves in a sidelong glance.

But this is a refugee camp, Saba blurted out. It is also a temporary place, our oasis until we leave.

The nomad nodded, smiling. Indeed, you are right.

The businessman asked Saba if she now would leave them alone.

Hajj Ali stood up and as he placed the cup in Saba's hand, he said: No harm in trying this place for some time. A heart needs its oasis too.

Outside, Saba leaned against the wall. Soon after, the men came out of the hut. Hajj Ali kneeled down to wash his face by the plastic water jug which stood against the wall of Saba's hut. Eyob grabbed the jug and poured water into the hands of the nomad man.

May God bless you, may God bless, Hajj Ali's voice boomed as he stood up. He fixed the sword dangling from his back. His daughter whistled twice. Almost immediately the herd moved, making the ground shake. Meat had arrived in the camp.

The nomad family set up their tents to the north of the camp, close to the river and the wilderness for their herd to roam about. A day after Hajj Ali's arrival, Saba went with Zahra to see him.

Saba waved at his wife and daughter who were building a makeshift barn at the bottom of a hill.

I just came to greet you, said Saba to the nomad.

Hajj Ali shook Saba's hand and praised God for the wisdom he had given to this young girl. Thank you for persuading us to stay, he said.

I thought it was the businessman who convinced him, Zahra said, as they walked back to the square.

I helped, Saba said. Her dimples deepened.

Everyone must know it then, said Zahra.

She held Saba by the hand and paused, bringing them to a halt on a steep pathway filled with bumps and cavities. They were surrounded by plants. A rabbit jumped over a shrub. Zahra closed her eyes and from memory she recited a passage from her mother's pamphlet: A woman is already forced to be invisible by men in our society, so she must amplify her contributions herself, no matter how small.

Saba didn't say anything.

So will you do it? asked Zahra. She did not wait for an answer, but ran down the path to the camp screaming: Because of Saba, Hajj Ali is staying. It wasn't just the businessman.

Saba laughed as she chased after her friend.

To bless his new, temporary base, Hajj Ali told Saba he was slaughtering three sheep.

With the help of young men, he brought the meat in three large flat straw baskets to the square. Women living nearby cooked the meat together and the square was turned into a communal eating area.

I hope to see you at my place, Hajj Ali said, through the judge's megaphone. I will sell milk and meat at affordable prices, God willing.

THE FIRST VIRGINITY TEST

It was early evening. The oil lamp wasn't outside the hut and Saba turned her torch off and waited behind the wall of Nasnet's kitchen until she was free. After what seemed a long time a man scurried out and away.

It's me, said Saba.

Nasnet opened the door and embraced Saba in the way she always did when they met, as if human warmth could be siphoned off like petrol. Nasnet pulled Saba to her bed and sat beside her.

I am happy you are here.

Saba smiled.

Your smile without the dimples on your cheeks is a false one, said Nasnet.

No one had noticed this about her before. But Saba didn't tell this to Nasnet.

There was a knock on the door.

Not now, Nasnet said from her bed. I am going to sleep.

Another knock.

Nasnet shuffled to the door and spoke through it: I said not now. Come tomorrow evening.

I want you now, said a man in a gruff voice.

It's Tedros, Nasnet said to Saba in a whisper. Come, hide.

Saba didn't move.

Nasnet grabbed her by the arm. Saba, you might think you know Tedros, but you have no idea what he is capable of when drunk. Here, go here, please. I will try to get rid of him.

With Saba under her bed, Nasnet walked back to the door. Please, come tomorrow, sweetheart, I am tired now, she said. What would a tired woman do for you?

Open, now. Or I'll break this door.

Okay, calm down, I am opening it, said Nasnet. Be gentle, okay, sweetheart.

From under the bed, Saba watched Tedros's Italian-made leather shoes, covered in dust, as he came into the hut and inched close to her face.

No, Tedros. You don't have to be aggressive to have a good time.

Shush, he said. Put this in your mouth. It will shut you up.

Tedros groaned. He dropped his shirt on the ground in front of Saba. The bed over her head creaked.

When he left, Saba staggered out from underneath her hiding place and took Nasnet into her arms. She hugged her. Nasnet was warm, her hair dishevelled. One of her earrings had popped off her ear. On her collarbone, Saba noticed a white trail, like a snake slithering at a languid pace to Nasnet's heart. Saba reached with her hands and fixed Nasnet's hair. She wiped the beads of sweat from her forehead. Scooped off the white snake by its tail. Wetting a towel with water from a jerrycan, she cleaned Nasnet's face.

Thank you, Saba, shokor.

Saba asked Nasnet to stand as she changed the bed linen that she had washed and ironed with the charcoal iron days earlier.

It's ready, said Saba. Come, sit.

Nasnet lay on her chest and stretched her arms, sinking deeper into the mattress. Saba sat by her side. Nasnet pulled back when Saba touched her shoulder.

The trick is to mentally transfer the pain to another part of your body, somewhere you can tolerate it, said Saba.

OK, Dr Saba, said Nasnet, chuckling.

Saba paused. Dr Saba, she mumbled to herself. Her dimples deepened. Returning her attention to Nasnet, she asked: Where does it hurt the most?

Nasnet guided Saba's hand to her legs, stopping between her thighs.

Saba separated Nasnet's legs. She didn't flinch, as if the act of looking was also a way of reclaiming Nasnet from Tedros, and from all the men before him. Saba blew her breath on Nasnet's vagina as Nasnet held her knees up. Then, she kissed it. And with her tongue she erased Tedros's presence.

Nasnet moaned.

Saba walked head down to the Khwaja for her English lesson. She paused now and then to look up at the sky as if to gather her thoughts, and take a deep breath. Boys ran past her. A father carried his daughter up the hill, piggyback. Faster Aboi, faster, the girl urged her father. Saba spotted a woman in conversation with the Khwaja outside his hut. So Saba lingered some distance away.

The Khwaja called his student over to him. Saba, Saba, come.

If it's too late, I can come tomorrow, she said to her teacher.

Time is irrelevant here, he said, putting on his glasses. Should we start?

Silence.

Saba, is everything fine? asked the Khwaja.

Have you ever been to see Nasnet? Saba asked.

The Khwaja turned up the wick of his oil lamp. No, he said, leaning back in his chair. I have never been to any sex worker in my life. He took a sip of his water. Trust me. Now, let's begin studying.

The Khwaja translated an article about animal welfare in the English countryside for her. This article, he said, contains useful words. After the horror of two wars, governments in the West are done with killing each other and now they are focused on stopping the murder of animals. They pass one law after another to protect their pets. We have a long way to go, Saba.

They might not be killing their people but they are helping the dergue kill us, Saba said. They say that the planes that flew over our town and the bombs they dropped were given by America and Russia. And do you know why they gave all that support to the dergue?

I do, said the Khwaja. I never heard you talk about this, but I do.

The Khwaja handed Saba a piece of paper. This evening, I want you to write sentences with words you've learnt so far.

Yes, I like this, said Saba, adding in English: Go let us.

The Khwaja chuckled. Indeed. Let us go would be more appropriate but not to worry for now. It will come.

Saba left the Khwaja's hut holding her piece of paper with her English writing which the Khwaja had said he would not correct for now.

Saba repeated her sentences as she headed home late at night. The midwife, who had left a pregnant woman's hut a few houses away from the Khwaja's, had seen Saba leaving his hut. Saba learnt this the following morning when she woke up to her mother's muttered objections: That is not possible, Saba is not like that.

Saba is at least seventeen, have you asked yourself why she hasn't had her period yet?

But not Saba. Saba is not like that.

Neighbours, accustomed to grieving, arrived to give their support. But they were turned away by the midwife. This was a different kind of death, Saba heard her tell them.

Saba wondered how many times she had died to her mother and the midwife at the exact moment she had felt herself alive. More than ever, I am not dead, she wanted to tell them. Touch me and see how my heart is beating.

Saba lay back on the blanket. She looked through the window, repeating some of the English words she had written down the previous night.

Not my Saba. Not my daughter. She is not like that.

Why else would a girl go into a man's hut at night, when a man is at his weakest?

Even though she heard them, even though she wanted to respond, defend herself that the only pleasure she had sucked out of the Khwaja was his knowledge of another language, Saba stayed silent. She did, though, notice the contrast between their Saba and her interpretation of herself. As if she had left her body and become another, Saba thought, when she observed herself from their perspective.

She wondered how the self could fragment and multiply into as many parts as the number of people observing it. Saba was Saba, but also a whore in the making, a ghost, a stubborn girl.

Please tell me, the mother said to the midwife. What can I do now? What will people say?

Saba left her mother's pleas behind her, and the midwife's suggestions for how to fix her daughter, and instead she imagined herself in a narrow, dark corridor of a university that smelt of books, of laboratories, studying in a classroom instead of being in a constant dream. Then – and how time flies in a dream – she walked out of the university building as Dr Saba.

Just then, the midwife and the mother restrained her. Saba kicked her legs about, trying to release herself from their grip. But to no avail. She stopped fighting. For a moment, and even as the midwife inserted her two fingers into Saba to test her virginity, to test that she hadn't slept with the Khwaja or any other man, calm ran through her. She realized how tired she was, how her body ached. She was exhausted from fighting. In that supine position, on her back, arms lifeless by her side, she felt at ease. Perhaps this was the natural position of a girl, she thought. If not, why did surrendering feel so much easier?

Days had passed since the midwife's fingers confirmed Saba's purity. Days since the mother ululated as if the midwife had delivered her new baby girl. Days since Saba found the comfortable position, on her back, her eyes shut without sleeping, when the world existed outside herself. She wasn't part of its advancement or destruction.

The blanket was warm and damp. The ground hard. The night wind filtered through the window bringing shrieks of crickets, like cracks of fire. Saba sat up and lit the oil lamp. To look away from her body now would have meant accepting the midwife's presence inside her for ever. It would have meant accepting the hurt, the intrusion, the growth of injustices like a thorn bush against her inner thighs. Saba decided to confront and to cleanse the ghost of the midwife. To liberate her body from the midwife and take it back. Like the flag of a free country, she planted pleasure on her assaulted body with her fingers.

A WOMAN

Saba stood outside the hut. She heard laughter as fresh as the morning as the young girls and boys hopscotched on the sandy ground. When she looked away from the children, Saba saw the businessman making his way to the office of the aid coordinator. He had yet to receive an answer to the request to allow the aid centre to provide loans to refugees and to speed up the issuing of travel permits.

Saba could picture the businessman trying to persuade the aid coordinator to do more to convince the regional authorities. She imagined him saying, After a while humans can't just survive on food and safety, even in a camp.

But maybe sometimes words have no power, Saba thought when she saw Tedros following his father into the aid centre, holding by its legs a rooster they had bought from Hajj Ali.

Saba felt a sudden pain in her back and tummy. As she placed a hand on her stomach, she felt something warm dripping down her leg.

Yikes! Look at Saba's legs, one of the girls behind her screamed.

The children scattered away. Saba looked down. Blood dripped down her leg to the grey earth beneath her. Saba ducked as the eagle swooped down on her blood.

The midwife took Saba inside and shut the door. Piercing ululations from her mother marked Saba's passage into womanhood, while the midwife folded a piece of cloth into a thick absorbent pad to place in Saba's underwear. Everything will be fine, sweetheart, now that you have become a woman, said the mother.

Saba expected womanhood, this phase of independence, to arrive once she was well on her way towards the goals she'd worked for at school, but it found her as a refugee in a camp. It was bewildering to her that a woman's passage into adulthood wasn't through her intellect, her character, but through her vagina. As far as she was concerned she had already been a woman for a long time now.

Saba clutched her stomach and sat on the blanket.

I will go and ask him to hurry up, said the midwife. Saba is not going to wait around forever now that she is a woman.

Saba sat up. When the midwife reached the door, she turned around. Tears welled up in her eyes. Her mother went up to the midwife. The two women hugged and wept.

Bringing up a girl is the ultimate responsibility God has placed on a parent, Saba remembered the midwife telling her mother after her father left when she was six. But I will help you, my sister. Saba is like my daughter. I will make sure she is brought up well.

Let me go to tell the businessman, said the midwife, freeing herself from the mother's embrace. No time to wait, she is ready.

That evening, though, it was another man who came asking for Saba's hand. He was not even the first. And like all those before him, he arrived with a gift.

Hajj Ali brought a plastic jug full of milk, mutton and eggs in a straw basket. Saba, though, knew her mother would turn him down, like the others. There was only one man in her mother's and the midwife's minds. A man with his own land back home, who would make the return, when it came, smoother.

She is still as strong as an ox, said the nomad of his wife's strength. But age hit her here, he dug his finger in his brown vest-clad chest. While the capacity to love in my heart swells with the passing of every day.

The mother asked Saba to wait outside the hut as she conversed with

Hajj Ali. Saba sat with Hagos next to the oil lamp that engraved an island of solitude around them. Brother and sister reunited in silence, like old times. How strange, Saba thought, that distance wedged between them while they lived in the same camp and the same hut, their blankets next to each other. It had been a long while since they had spent time with each other in the way they used to.

Eyob had come between them, she thought. He gave her a job, and the possibility to dream again, while at the same time he provided Hagos with a friendship he had never had. Eyob gave her and Hagos the chance to have some space from each other in this confined place. Saba remembered what Zahra had said. To see is not the same as to be seen. That was what kept her sane, how she managed mentally to create a distance for herself, by merely pretending at times to ignore others. And even herself.

Saba drew her feet up and hugged her legs. But you are a traveller, Hajj Ali, her mother's response came through the window. Saba had never heard her mother speak with such confidence.

You might not realize it, but you are all eternal travellers, Hajj Ali responded. People from a place with continuous violence seek oases like nomads.

Hagos stood up. Saba followed him with her eyes as he paced up and down. He picked up a stick and sat in front of her. He tried to talk. Saba leaned forward. His cheeks inflated. Words stuck in his mouth and his tears fell. Saba wiped at her brother's face until clarity returned to his eyes. She tried to read the reason for his rage in them, understand his burst of emotion.

Saba was born into his universe of silence. Hagos was simple, everyone told her. Innocent and without mystery. Like everyone else, she didn't want to pretend otherwise and disturb the peace that he brought into her life. She had trusted her body with him because of his God-given innocence. Her legs lengthened, her breasts grew in front of this man who had the gullibility of a child.

And this Hagos, the Hagos she imagined him to be, the Hagos she constructed in her mind, could not be a lie. He was as real as she and everyone else made him to be. Shokor Hagos. But sweet Hagos wanted to write now. He stabbed the ground with the stick, inscribing fury instead of words.

Hagos, no, she said. No.

He jabbed the ground with his stick again. The whipped-up sand filled Saba's throat. She coughed.

Hagos turned around and leaned against the wall. He dropped his head between his knees.

Saba scrawled letters in the sand, hoping the wind would not blow. Come, she said, holding his hand. Come, let's begin. We will both learn a new language. First, I'll teach you the little I know. We will both start at the same level. No one better than the other.

She read and reread every letter of the English alphabet out loud as she scribbled it in the sand. Hagos stared at the letters, then at Saba's lips, then back at the letters on the moonlit ground. Saba put Hagos's hand in hers. She guided her older brother to write his first word. First phrase. Register his footprint in the soil of the camp in English, a language that would be his first, as good as the tongue that abandoned him. Together they wrote their names:

HAGOS
SABA

The businessman emerged from the crowded square. He stood in front of the siblings.

When the mother came out of the hut and saw Eyob, she embraced him. The businessman clasped his hands and said to Saba's mother: The midwife came to see me, but I think there is a misunderstanding.

He unwrapped the gabi from around his neck. He sighed and took the mother's hand. Please understand, he said, kissing the back of her hand again and again. Saba is still young and despite what you heard, it was never my intention to marry her.

People gasped. Why then did you befriend the mute? the athlete asked, drawing himself out of the crowd.

Mr Eyob, her mother said, her voice audible to all. Mr Eyob, but you also need to understand that people have been talking. They see you come here every evening, bringing gifts, and they wonder why a middle-aged man, who is rich and from Asmara, would befriend a young man who is a poor countryside boy and mute.

Eyob brought his hands together in front of his chest again. I am sorry if I gave you and everyone else in this camp the wrong impression. But–

But what, Mr Eyob? asked her mother. Saba is a woman now and I want to protect her reputation. Honour is what we have left. I urge you not to come here again.

Saba followed the businessman's eyes as they settled on Hagos. Hagos's hair quivered in the breeze. It was as if the moon and stars shone only for him. It was as if everyone else around him vanished. Eyob took a deep breath. Okay, he said to the mother, without looking away from Hagos. As you wish. I would like to ask for Saba's hand.

That night, Saba listened to Hagos weeping until he fell into a restless sleep. The following morning, she opened her eyes to his stare, eyes that showed the same anger she remembered from those early days of her school life. Red eyes that pursued her as she washed her face, combed her hair, ate breakfast, put her books in her bag, and then walked to the gate and turned towards him to wave goodbye.

Good morning, Hagos-ay, Saba said, now sitting up on her blanket. Adding the -ay, attaching Hagos to her, mine, my Hagos, mine like the air, mine like the skin around my bones. She was engaged but nothing was going to change between them. She wanted to tell him this, if he only would sit and let her talk to him.

Many nights of crying, many silent mornings followed. And one morning, Hagos waited for her to wake up, a pen and paper in his hands.

Do you want to continue our English lessons? Saba asked.

He nodded, his head moving up and down in a rapid jerk, as if, Saba thought, a language could be learnt that fast.

Let's eat first, the mother said.

Hagos shook his head.

He hasn't been eating for days now. Don't you want to eat? Saba asked.

Hagos, though, put the pen and paper in her hand. Okay, let's start then, Saba said, leaving her own breakfast untouched.

And when Hagos returned later that evening, he hurried past Saba and lay on his blanket, facing the wall without changing or taking off his shoes.

Saba turned up the wick of the lamp. It was raining outside, yet Hagos was barely wet, as if he'd been sheltered during his walk.

The silence inside the hut was broken by the occasional rumble in the sky. Saba sat up and pulled out the painting from Hagos's jute sack and leaned against the wall. The closer she looked at the portrait this time, the more Saba discovered similarities between the white woman and herself. All the time it hung on her wall back home, all the time she held it in this camp ever since she discovered it, all this and it never occurred to her that this might have been her. That it could have been Hagos and not the landlord who'd painted this portrait. And that Hagos disguised her under an unblemished white skin.

But the square face, the dimples on the cheeks, the long neck, the long, narrow almond eyes, the broad shoulders, the slender breasts, the wide hips all resembled her, Saba. The white skin was diversion, a buffer against possible accusations that a man had dared to paint his own sister naked.

THE BROKEN LANGUAGE

WHEN YOU LEARN A LANGUAGE AS AN ADULT, WORDS ARE LIKE RAZORS ON YOUR TONGUE. THE SENTENCES YOU SPEAK ARE SO WOUNDED THAT THEY FALL APART WHEN THEY LEAVE YOUR MOUTH.

remember this i well   hagos me fight had   hagos do run   follow i him
field of landlord arrive   sorghum tall me as   clouds sudden come   rain
see i hagos run here there   follow him i   find he room to our landlord
belong hagos in go   to window go i take look high shelves everywhere
books big   now see i why this room close always   no one in come
workers told were   hagos wet clothes off take   on chair put he   book lift
this book notice i no words has pictures only   cry want i   never hagos
see happy as this   when i sudden voice hear   degas name is   hagos fell
book to floor   look for his clothes   no wait say landlord   at book by
hagos feet point he   on page open is woman like hagos naked   see say
landlord degas this paint   i this painting see in paris   i hereafter painter
want become   and wish i woman habesha paint like her me let   eyes of
hagos rest on woman in bucket bath landlord hagos hand holding still
but say he landlord no girl from here find i who this accept   all say no
to hagos the landlord say this hagos i teach you paint really no need be

literate or speak   to draw but if i paint like this you me let   hagos down head   think landlord hand of hagos go let   sorry say he   how ask this could i of another man   i no do this again   hagos landlord hand back grab   nod he   you me let paint you   hagos nod landlord cry   i cry   i watch hours   as landlord hagos paint   hagos me think learnt paint how so he me paint   see this nude white me is   hide me black in skin of Europe   us free become think i when hide not art   one day hagos paint me   as me is   black with all wounds

FREE LOVE, FENCED

Saba and Hagos joined a crowd watching a group of men fencing off Eyob's three huts with thorn bush. Lightning flashed across the dark sky and Saba spotted Jamal on top of the hill. He was surrounded by oil lamps. She could see him clearly.

Next to Jamal, the large white sheet tied to two poles blew in the wind, like a flag of surrender to passion, to that impossible desire that she, as many, were taught to never recognize, let alone express.

Why is he building this fence? asked a man behind Saba. She looked away from Jamal and brought her attention to Eyob's new fence.

It is not as if we are wild cattle that he needs to keep at bay, said a man, kicking at the fence made of thorn bush with his shoe. Maybe he has a secret to hide.

The brother and sister stood in front of the gate. The workers left. Eyob sat on his chair. Oil lamps lit up the compound, making it look like an oasis of light bathing in a sea of darkness.

Soon she would live in this compound. Hagos too. It was Saba's only condition for accepting Eyob's proposal. She didn't want a dowry. She wanted Hagos. His presence around me is worth more to me than a gold ring on my finger, Saba wanted to tell them. He is a crown on my head, a lush white dress around my body. His smooth skin is mine in place of what you burnt on me. He is my peace that you took away. He is not forbidden, because as the religious men had said, he's heaven and in heaven all is allowed.

Hagos smiled his quiet smile. But Saba could hear a storm between his ribs as the bones of his chest strained when he hugged her.

How could she have underestimated the impact of their separation on him, even if she was only moving from one part of the camp to another? They were twins. Born from the same womb in different years but bound together by circumstances, the war between their parents' countries and the one waged on their bodies.

Yes, it would be my absolute pleasure, indeed, if Hagos moves in with us, Eyob said, promising to build a new hut for Hagos.

But when Saba requested a fence be built, the businessman raised his eyebrows as his eyes scanned Saba, as if lost in a maze of thoughts. Saba curbed the temptation to explain the need for confinement within a confined camp, for exile within exile. There was no need. The businessman would understand in time.

Okay, he said. If you want a compound, I'll set it up.

And here, in this compound, Saba would live with her husband, Hagos and Tedros. All the huts next to each other. Fenced. At the foot of a hill, where Jamal had started constructing his cinema.

Tedros emerged from their new latrine, a hole in the ground located at the back of the compound. Saba followed him with her eyes as he fetched a towel from the clothesline and strode behind a small wall made of thatch, sewn with ropes, the gaps blanked out with l eaves. Complete privacy. Only God could see this shower room from above.

In weeks, after her wedding, she too would disappear with a bucket of water into that tiny shower room, on her own. She had long craved moments like these. When she stood instead of hunching up inside a bucket. She imagined her wet body under the sky, the direct sun, the wind, the rain, the stars and the moon.

Soapy water streamed from under the thatched wall of the shower room. Tedros came out with a towel wrapped around his waist. He jumped over a puddle and stuttered into the hut without a glance at the throng outside the compound.

Saba waved back at Eyob, at the same time as her brother, as if the businessman's wave was intended for both, as if he too finally understood that they were each other's double, two who only made sense together.

THE WHITE CLOTH

Saba arrived in the area north of the camp. Hajj Ali's daughter pastured their animals on the grass of the hill. His wife stirred a pot over a stove with one hand while shaking a goatskin bag tied between two logs with the other. Her eyes were half closed as if in deep contemplation.

The smell of butter hung in the air. Saba greeted the woman with narrow eyes, the woman whose own husband had described to her mother as empty of love. The woman, though, stood up and hugged Saba, pouring into her ear words that had aged with the milk she fermented in her travels: Love, my daughter, is the cradle in which our wisdom churns.

As Saba was about to leave with three eggs and a spoonful of butter that she paid for with her earnings at Eyob's, Hajj Ali held her hand. And tell the idle businessman I will come soon to see him, he said.

She nodded, freeing her fingers from his grasp.

I am not sure a husband like him is capable of doing anything except taking evening walks, said the nomad, laughing. That's not what a young woman needs.

Saba turned to look at his wife, who had again closed her eyes, returning to her daydream as her hands worked, rocking side to side, as if she was cradling her lonely heart.

Evening. Full moon. Twinkling stars. Music bellowed from a small radio outside Azyeb's bar. Saba sat behind the shrub and peered through its leaves. The drinkers sat under a hanging oil lamp.

Tedros started another jar of tej against the pleas of Azyeb. You are going to kill yourself, the barwoman urged him. Stop.

Leave him, said the praise poet. His father asked him to be his best man at his wedding to Saba, his sweetheart.

How cruel, said the athlete. Fathers know children can't say no to them.

Tedros took a piece of white cloth from his shirt pocket. Saba bowed and she thought of the night to come in a few days, when Tedros would pass this white cloth to his father before they entered their marital bedroom, a test of the bride's virtue. Saba wondered if she had enough blood left inside her to mark the white cloth.

Forget Saba, the athlete said to Tedros. Go to Mariam. I heard, my dear gentlemen, that since her divorce she's been giving it away for free.

We call her the aid centre, said the praise poet, laughing.

I think she married that man so she could get it over with, said the athlete. Now she no longer has her virginity to guard, she can live as she always wanted.

Actually, said the praise poet, her husband said she came to him spoiled.

How does he know? Azyeb asked.

Well, said the praise poet, the poor man couldn't draw blood out of her.

Why are men so obsessed with a woman's blood? said Azyeb. Not all women bleed the first time. I didn't and nor did my sister. Or my cousin. Girls' livelihoods are being destroyed because of your failure to understand.

A woman is too complex for a man, said Jamal. That's why we reduce her to simple matters.

No, said Azyeb. It shows how much violence there is against women, if even love has to be equated with drawing blood from a woman.

Azyeb fanned her open furnace. The charcoal embers glowed. Saba squinted.

Haleeb haleeb haleeb.

The voice of Hajj Ali's daughter, selling milk, rang out.

Tedros called the girl carrying a pot of milk on her head over to him.

Are you going to drink milk and beer? asked the athlete.

A man's wounded heart needs a cocktail of extreme variety to survive a moment like this, said the praise poet.

THE DANCE

Saba entered the camp from the forest carrying firewood one afternoon, and paused outside Jamal's hut. The entertainer was behind a large white screen planting a wild yellow hibiscus tree. The twigs of wood that Saba had tied to her back with a scarf squeaked as she sped away. When she arrived at the bottom of the hill, she stood on her toes and peeked over the thorn fence of Eyob's compound. Men were painting blue the mud wall of the new hut the businessman had built for Hagos. Her brother's hut was to be filled with furniture Eyob had bought from Nasnet. Hagos's new bed would be the bed of the sex worker. The bed with the thick mattress that Nasnet brought with her when she was evicted from the city because the comfort of being on top of that material compensated for the duress of being under the weight of a man. Nasnet got a cheap angareb – a wooden framed bedstead – as a gift from one of the aid workers instead.

Once home, Saba dropped her load by the mogogo stove and went inside the hut. She leaned against the door frame and buried her head in her hands, her lips resting on her bruised palms.

Saba heard a bleating. She looked through the window. Tedros stood holding a goat on a leash. The white cloth – the imminent test of her purity that he carried with him around the camp – popped out of his shirt pocket.

I bought this from Hajj Ali, he said, caressing the black and white animal. It's for your wedding.

I no longer eat meat, Saba said.

You will soon be the meat for my father, he said, sniggering.

Saba gathered her saliva and spat into his face. The goat pawed the ground, kicking up clouds of dust. You will pay for this, Tedros said, wiping the side of his face with the white cloth.

He pulled the goat behind him as he left. When Saba sat inside the bucket for a bath, some of the water splashed out onto the floor. As she squeezed inside that tiny place, her body felt as suffocated as her soul, and her dreams felt trapped in this camp. Saba shuffled in the bucket, the water underneath tickling her skin. Out of the thatched roof, a moth descended. It rested on her chest, its wings spread on her breast. When Saba stepped out of the bucket, the moth soared away through the window. As she loosened the towel around her hips, she noticed papers scattered on Hagos's blanket, papers on which she had written and taught him what she in turn had learnt from the Khwaja.

Saba sat on her stool outside the hut in the moon-bathed square. She had seen the scene in front of her many times before. Every day was a repetition of the previous one in this camp. Still, she observed what was unfolding in front of her, intrigued as though it were her first encounter. Saba couldn't imagine doing otherwise. Couldn't let boredom set in. So she smiled as she watched children racing each other, the athlete playing football with a sock ball, taking the opportunity to ogle Samhiya, painting her nails by the sideline, with every pause in the game. And when a dance began around the singer in a slow, endless circle, it seemed to Saba that their country's dance was conceived in response to their history, marred by repetition of the same bloodied story over and over again.

Come and join us, people urged each other.

Let's dance. Let's dance.

Saba took a stroll and found herself outside Jamal's hut. The entertainer was sitting with the two old men, the Asmarinos in colourful cardigans and Zahra's grandmother. The cinema-screen sheet, with a big square cut out in the middle, quivered behind them in the breeze. On the screen, the bees buzzed on the yellow flowers of the hibiscus tree, beginning the process of reproduction.

The grandmother called Saba over. Come and join us, she said. We are talking about love.

Among other things, said the white-haired man in a blue cardigan, laughing.

Anyway, she is too young to join our conversation, said the bald, clean-shaven man wearing a pink jumper.

She is the same age as Jamal, said the grandmother. But it seems to you a woman has to be double the age of a man before she matches his wisdom.

Exactly, said the man in the blue cardigan.

The man in pink nodded and, turning towards Saba, he said, Signorina, I am too old to stand up unaided. Please come and help me.

How come this grandmother here would need no help and she is older than you? said the man in the blue cardigan.

It is not the years that weigh one down, said the man in pink, but the numbers of lovers in one's heart.

The grandmother laughed. The weight of the one true love I had would outweigh all your encounters.

After she helped him to stand up, the old man bowed his head at Saba and kissed her hand. Signorina, forgive this foolish old man for assumptions unnecessarily made under the duress of bad company.

All this effort to say a simple thing, said the man in the blue cardigan.

Indeed, said the man in pink. I am a man of my time, and in our time, we treated women like goddesses.

Just treat us like human beings, said the grandmother, and that would solve the world's problems.

Saba sat down next to the grandmother, who took her hand. Anyway, let me go back to what I was saying, she said. The power of love erases all differences. It humanizes us and brings our energies, spiritual and physical, to one combined force. When we make love, we are meant to be one.

The two old men shook their heads. Sciocchezza!

Turning to Saba and Jamal, the grandmother asked, And how about you? What do you think about love and its fruits that ripen in the bodies of lovers?

And now she is asking these two? said the man in pink. They don't even know how babies are made.

The two men chuckled.

Saba and Jamal exchanged glances before looking away from each other.

Ignore these old men, said the grandmother to Saba and Jamal. But for fairness, just as the old impart their wisdom, the youth must share the lyrics of their fantastical imaginations with the old.

What are we going to do with these? asked the man in blue. At our age, what one needs is more sleep, not excess alertness.

The man in pink lit a cigarette that he passed to the grandmother. Do the honour of passing the flame of love to the next generation then, Mebrat, he said.

The grandmother took a long drag, to satisfy her young heart, she said, before passing the cigarette to Jamal.

Jamal, tell me, said the grandmother. And don't be shy, I have heard it all. As a farmer, I have sown the seeds of desire in my skin at the same time as I planted my land with pumpkin seeds.

Saba turned to Jamal when she noticed him staring at her. He looked away quickly. He hooked a foot around the stool, put his hand inside his pocket and took it out again.

I can't say now, Jamal said, his voice shaking.

I hope I will be alive when you are ready to talk, said the grandmother, chuckling.

Jamal scrambled to his feet and went around to stand behind the white sheet.

Let me tell you this story, said the grandmother. On my wedding night, when we retreated to our bedroom, my husband dimmed the light and stood naked in front of me. He expected to jump on me. I said to him, I want a lover. So I made him lick my toes that night. And my fingers the next evening. And the third night he spent discovering the length and width of my back. Like this I made him make love to every bit of me. There is no virginity, I told him. No one is a virgin only once. With every new lover, we turn virgin again. Because it is not a hole you make love to but a body, a mind and a heart. And I did the same. I remember when I parted his buttocks, how he protested, God bless his soul. You don't fuck me. We fuck each other, I said to him. To be honest, he dropped his guard with one gentle stroke. Men are like that, they have no idea of the treasures on their bodies. If they did, they would not go around forcing women with violence.

The grandmother and the men left soon after, but Saba stayed behind. She tilted her head and observed Jamal, who stood behind the makeshift screen sheet. It was like watching a film in the way he appeared to her through the square hole on the white sheet. It was strange to her that it was she who fed his desires. She could see it in the softness of his skin, the lean shape of his body.

Saba felt the urge to enter the screen and reach Jamal, fulfil his fantasy because it was hers too. And as she stood up and put one leg through the screen – the cinema yet to open its doors to the public – her body shook as if she was back on top of the camel during her journey to the camp. Come, said Jamal, extending his hand towards Saba. Come. Saba. Sabbina. Come.

I still recall that summer evening inside Cinema Silenzioso when a naked Saba crouched on my face. My eyes travelled across the long back of this woman I had loved since the first night in the camp. Above her arched neck, the stars glimmered around the moon. The call to the last prayer of the day was being announced via the plastic megaphone.

Saba rearranged herself, spreading her map of love over me.

This is our time, she said. This is my time.

I wanted to speak but I was breathless.

Saba caressed my face as I inhaled the scent of her, the scent of her history, the battles she had won and lost, her rage, her frustrated dreams, the violence on her thighs, the rivers of desire inside her womb.

She let go.

She filled my mouth from her rivers, so warm that as it slid inside me through my throat, I felt riches invading me, gushing towards my soul, the White Nile and its water running between my ribs.

The strings of the singer's krar played a mournful song nearby. The forest whistled. That impious breeze of the summer wafted against my cheeks. Like a famished soul, I tried to grasp the warm air, my hands fluttering at my sides. Saba pushed down with her weight, screwing the lock of my existence to her being even more. North and south finally reunited, Saba erasing the boundaries that have separated us for so long.

THE GOAT

A lizard scurried across Eyob's compound and up the wall of the kitchen hut. Saba gathered her hair and tied it into a knot at her nape. Her silhouette curved against the bundle of coloured clothes she'd yet to wash. She dipped her hands into the bucket and washed Eyob's gabi. The goat bleated. It jumped and kicked. Tedros stormed out of his hut, with the white cloth still tucked into his shirt pocket. He screamed at the animal: Shut up, I need to sleep.

The goat continued its bleating. Tedros flung himself towards it and knocked it to the ground with a punch. Saba jumped over the bucket and rushed to the animal. Tedros grabbed her by her arm and dragged her inside the latrine.

Remember the spit on my face because of that goat? You will now pay for it. I am going to spoil you before my father even touches you.

Do it. The wedding night will be interesting when the white cloth you carry remains white and your guests have nothing to celebrate.

I always knew you were a slut. Just like my mother.

I will be your stepmother in days.

So you are happy to marry an old man for his money. Here, have a look at this, he said, pulling down his trousers. You will never see its equivalent.

I have seen it, Saba said. Masturbating while you scream my name.

Tedros spat at her.

We are even now, said Saba. Let me go, stepson.

Stop calling me that.

And you stop holding my neck.

Tedros turned her around. Now, I can have your other hole and nobody, not even my father, will know I had you. I heard you girls love doing it before your wedding, anyway. It's probably as big as your mouth.

It is for your small dick.

I am not small.

Saba laughed.

Tedros pushed Saba aside and stormed out of the latrine. When she hurried outside, Saba saw Tedros approaching the goat, a knife in his hand.

Fuck your wedding, I will kill it now, he said.

He wrestled the goat to the ground. The animal's cries fell to gurgles as Tedros slit its throat. Blood splattered everywhere. The white cloth in his pocket turned red. He turned the goat on its back and cut off its testicles and said, his voice rising so that his father, inside his hut, would hear every word: Here, feed these to Hagos so he can get some balls on him.

Tedros threw the bloodied white cloth at Saba and said, Wash it and iron it properly. I want it back as good as new for your wedding night.

CINEMA SILENZIOSO

Saba's eyes rested on the white screen and the coloured plastic chair inside it. Behind the chair, the camp bathed under the bright sky. The smoke of firewood rose between the randomly dotted huts and coiled around the thatched roofs. Hurry up, start the show, boys, urged Jamal. But the show had already begun. Anyone could enter the screen and sit under the moon and the stars to sing, dance, talk, fall silent, tell a story, reminisce, undress, dress, shave, do whatever he, she or they wanted. But no one moved.

A gust of wind blew through the camp. The audience kept their heads up, as if they were watching a storm in a film made somewhere else. Saba squinted as the yellow dust of the square and the red dust of the hills intermingled and rose above the thatched roofs of the huts. She observed the disappearance of the camp in the cinema. For a moment, the camp existed in sound and smell only. The cacophony made it appear that the opera singer, the first of them to die in the camp, had risen from her grave. Her ghost danced through the wind. This camp was singing her presence from beyond the grave.

Silence. Until a man in blue overalls stepped inside the cinema. He danced. His hands stretched here and there, as if he were the wave of the Red Sea, of their country's sea, bringing its riches to their laps in exile. One might leave a country, said the dancer, but a country never leaves you.

He inhaled and exhaled. Saba smelt stale sardines on his breath.

The next performer, a boy, stood inside the screen, his face gaunt, his eyes half closed. Saba remembered him. He was the boy she had seen in the square on the first night, with a baby strapped to his back. His back was empty now. But he still hunched forward, as if carrying his little brother, he still rocked as if he wanted to put him to sleep. Please sleep my sweet little brother, he sang. Please sleep.

From his pocket, the boy pulled out a balloon that, he said, his father had bought for him as he sent him and his brother to safety after the death of their mother.

As he blew up the balloon, his cheeks inflated. Fattening on his brother's memory. A gush of wind pulled the balloon out from the clutch of his lips, launching it into the sky of the camp. The same sky which, after many long months saturated with the pollution of grief, began to clear in patches, normality appearing in pockets, while sadness like potholes continued to be scattered everywhere.

After a lull, Tedros stuttered forward with a jug in his hand. The screen wobbled as he entered through the gap in the sheet rather than going round the back. He sat down on the coloured chair, his red eyes piercing through the screen. Saba didn't blink.

This is not fair, he said. He paused. Taking a sip of his beer, he wagged his finger at the audience: The world forgot us, you say, but we too forgot each other. To survive in this place you have to forget your humanity.

For a drunk person, you are wise, said a spectator, bringing laughter to the cinema.

Tedros picked a yellow flower from the hibiscus tree next to him and put it into his pocket next to the white cloth. He breathed in, his chest expanded. His arms slumped by his side. His jug fell. A splash of beer hit Saba's arm through the screen. He sang a love song:

Saba Sabina, Saba Sabina, Saba Sabina, Saba Sabina
Aney wey aney, Aney wey aney

His voice trailed off. Behind Tedros, Saba could see the businessman's compound at the foot of the hill. Saba jumped to her feet.

Sit down, spectators shouted at Saba from behind.

Did the rest of the audience witness the setting of a story yet to be told? Saba wondered. And as she sat back, she noticed her brother and the businessman entering the compound. Hagos, Saba mumbled. The two men sat on Eyob's bed outside. Hagos's beaming face overshadowed everything around it. Perhaps it was because of him that Jamal had set his cinema in that spot, Saba thought. Why else, she wondered to herself, did Jamal call his cinema Cinema Silenzioso? Hagos, the silent man who never uttered a word, yet could captivate the audience with his mere presence. A Signora, at attore cinematografico.

But this cinema was another way to tell a story rooted in their tradition, their life. What she was watching was reality, not a film made in the West. What was unfolding before her eyes in the compound she was staring at through the cinema was part of her own life, made in the camp. Two Habesha men gazing at each other, two Habesha men who intertwined their fingers as they kissed in Cinema Silenzioso.

THE MAP OF THE COUNTRY

The morning after the opening of the cinema, Saba was at Eyob's compound. She dipped her hands into the bucket full of Tedros's clothes from the previous night. Hajj Ali came through the gate holding a gift.

Saba bumped the bucket as she stood up to welcome him. Water spilt over the clothes she was about to wash, the ones her fiancé and his best man were to wear on the wedding night.

This is my gift to your man, said Hajj Ali. His hand rested on hers, heavy like a rock, as he handed her a bag of meat.

Where is the businessman? he asked.

Saba pulled her hand away. He is resting, she said.

A businessman who seeks rest has forfeited his calling, Hajj Ali said, laughing. Our hope rests in you. When will you reopen the shop?

Soon, Saba said. Adding, as if to calm his impatience, God willing.

Indeed, in Him we trust, said Hajj Ali, clapping his hands and calling on Eyob to come out. Get up and show this young lady your vitality, old man.

By the time the businessman emerged in his tunic, Saba had prepared tea.

Eyob didn't talk, as if, when he kissed Hagos the night before, he had swallowed all the silence on her brother's tongue.

Finally, Hajj Ali put an end to this silence by revealing information about the village he and his family had stayed in before they arrived at the camp. Information he'd been withholding since his arrival. His eyes on Saba, he said, Although it took us a long time to get here with the animals, I would say it is ten hours by foot. I am sure as a businessman yourself, brother Eyob, you will agree with me that in a camp like this, every piece of knowledge about the outside world is priceless.

Saba, though, was certain Eyob no longer wanted to leave the camp, escape its remoteness, its scarcity, now that he had found love that grew in a camp, love he couldn't find at his villa in Asmara, in his own country. Hajj Ali's information was for her.

Saba raised her eyes above the bucket with dirty clothes, looking at the man who had asked for her hand before Eyob.

What a village it is, brother Eyob. It has a fantastic school.

Saba slowed the movement of her hands. So the village is only ten hours away? the businessman asked, in a whisper. Really? Saba was sure that he had conveyed a note of excitement only out of politeness.

Yes. Maybe a bit more, said Hajj Ali. But this village is reachable with His grace, and the rest of this country and even the world is accessible from that point on.

Hajj Ali smiled at Saba. Her mind, though, was occupied by the same thing that enlivened her heart, the thing that had kept her awake at night back home. What does it take for a dream to die? Saba wondered to herself.

I thought the next town was so far away that it wasn't even worth thinking about, said Eyob. But that is what happens when they drop you here in the middle of the night.

Tedros came into the compound with a jug of beer. He had slept at Azyeb's bar. Is the white cloth ready? he asked Saba. We will need it tomorrow.

He was drinking his life away because he had lost her, but he never had her in the first place, Saba thought. Yet he was grieving over love he had conceived in his head and had imagined would be reciprocated.

Tedros picked up the white cloth from the pile by Saba's feet and threw it into the bucket. Saba looked at her fiancé. Eyob shuffled on his stool. Some time passed in silence before Hajj Ali brought the conversation back to the village, pressing the same point that was of interest to Saba.

And, Hajj Ali continued, before I came here, they apparently opened the new road that connects the village to the capital, with the best university on our continent. So no one here with the ambition to finish their education should let distance discourage them, not with this new road. The future is bright. But we all have to pay a price to be part of it.

Hajj Ali took a sip of his tea and asked Eyob for something to scribble on. With his request answered, the nomad stretched out his leg and placed the paper on his lower thigh, as close as possible to Saba, and drew a map of his country. He located the camp with the tip of his pencil. Here, he said, that's where we live.

Saba examined the map and the dot that represented the camp. And that pencil-scrawled point was enough to make her feel that the place where she lived counted. This camp was part of something. And she was too.

Hajj Ali was about to crumple the paper into a ball when Saba asked to have it. He smiled. With pleasure, he said.

With the paper in Saba's hands, the nomad addressed Eyob. What is the use of a permanently closed shop? Maybe we should arrange a trip to the village to get some products. You need to work. A businessman without work is like a man in a marriage without sex.

He laughed. And his laughter continued until he drew Saba out of her reverie. She looked up, as if to say I understand, no more inference is needed.

Men are easy to read.

Sadly, we have been told we are not authorized to leave the camp without a permit, said Eyob.

You seem to forget that I am from this country, Eyob. And as a citizen, I am your permit. And no one else in this camp knows the way. Hajj Ali looked at Saba as he repeated this fact a few times. Saba knew. He began bargaining, for something that had nothing to do with business.

And I have a cart, said Hajj Ali.

A cart?

Yes, Eyob. I made one. I bought the wheels from the aid lorry drivers and built the body part using trees from the wood. It should do the job, God willing. And it will cut the trip to eight hours. But given that I own the transport, that I will be your permit and your guide, then, I am sure you agree this is something very invaluable indeed. No amount of money can compensate for it.

Saba withdrew her hands from the water and sat straight, staring at the herder who could no longer distinguish between meat and her body.

Well, Eyob, said Hajj Ali, sleep on it and let me know tomorrow if you can find something to excite me so I can do this trip on that inhospitable road for your sake. Or for anyone else in your household.

The businessman returned to his hut. Hajj Ali leaned forward towards Saba. I will wait for you, he said. My price is reasonable when it's your future at stake.

Once back at her hut, Saba lodged a piece of wood inside a crevice in the mud wall and hung the map on it, above her blanket.

THE WEDDING

Ululations erupted around the hut and continued as Saba emerged in her wedding dress. She held Hagos's hand, and together they set off to Eyob. Her mother, the midwife and the guests clapped and danced as they followed behind Saba. Through the sand she dragged the hem of the white dress that had belonged to a woman who was now dead.

She ambled past children writing on each other's arms with charcoal, using their skins instead of paper. The English aid coordinator, on his way back to his base with his assistant after a day spent in the camp, applauded when he saw her.

Saba paused her march and said to him in English: When school come?

The Englishman smiled. We are doing our best, he said.

His assistant laughed. Anyway, you don't need school. Look at you, English speaker.

The aid workers smiled as they got into their Land Rover and drove off.

Saba sat on an armchair next to her husband. Women presented the husband's gift to her. The luggage contained lingerie, bras, blouses, shirts, earrings, necklaces, a wristwatch - most of these Saba had seen on Nasnet and spotted other girls wearing around the camp. Saba knew it was Hagos who had chosen every item.

The party began.

The singer mounted a table and played her krar. Saba raised her eyes above the dancing circle. She spotted Jamal on his hill. No doubt he was watching the wedding through the screen of his cinema, Saba thought, as if it were held in a faraway land, a romantic wedding, concluding a treacherous life of war and exile.

The singer began the last song of the night, blessing the wedding, wishing the bride and groom a long life of love, happiness and prosperity.

Saba was about to follow her husband into their marital hut when she noticed Tedros positioning himself by the window. The pretence of tradition has no limits, she thought. The front of his trousers barely held back his erection. She knew he'd rather be in the bed in his father's place than outside by the window. Saba no longer wondered what it was about her that stirred him so. It was about ownership. He was speaking to her through an unwritten language: that he could shove the length of his manhood inside her, break her spine to replace it with his own, so that she stood and fell at his behest. And Saba wondered for how long it would be contained, how long before he carried out his threat to induce an irreversible damage. He crumpled up the white cloth. The door closed. The music outside stopped.

In the glow of an oil lamp by the bed that Saba was to share with Eyob, she examined the time that never mattered, but that was now tied to her wrist on a watch given to her by her husband. It was seven minutes past midnight. Saba went out into the compound. Chairs, plates and cups were scattered everywhere. The remnants of the wedding party drifted in the wind. When she looked up, she saw Tedros sitting on a stool outside his hut, an oil lamp by his side. A jug rolled on the ground by his foot. The smell of alcohol filled the air. He staggered to his feet and fiddled with the piece of white cloth. He laughed, the same laughter that she thought made him more attractive when she first heard it. He left the compound.

The cloud thickened. The moon disappeared. The gate flapped. It was a gust of wind. Saba sighed and raised her head towards the hill. The screen of Cinema Silenzioso remained in place.

Back inside the hut from the latrine, Saba took off her pyjamas, one of her wedding gifts. She stretched on the bed next to her husband and kept her eyes locked on the window until the sunrise emerged from behind the clouds. Her watch showed six. She broke into pieces the bread she had baked on the mogogo stove to make kitcha fetfit and put it in a bowl for her husband who sat on the chair next to her.

Tedros came out of his hut and sat on his stool without greeting his father. He took the white cloth out of his pocket and fiddled with it, as if he'd meant to land a blow on his father with each touch. Saba wondered how Eyob restrained himself. He must have seen this thing his son used as a weapon against him, because her supposed impurity reflected on her husband as much as it did on her. Yet Eyob neither said nor did anything. He was, Saba was sure, aware Tedros was waving it outside the camp like a white flag, a sign of his father's capitulation to a woman's promiscuous past.

Saba poured tea for Eyob. Hagos left his blue hut and watered the flowers he had harvested weeks before from the wild and replanted by the door of his hut. Bees buzzed around him. Hagos's face looked as captivating as the yellow, red and white jasmines. He had found his place, Saba thought. His paradise.

Hagos returned to his hut, leaving behind the bees which had abandoned their hives to congregate at his turf. Eyob took two cups of tea and the bowl of bread with berbere and butter that Saba had prepared, saying he was going to have his breakfast with Hagos. She watched him tread through the compound to the blue hut as if he were stepping on an imaginary rope hanging up in the air. This will take some time to get used to, Saba thought. She looked up at the cinema and wondered if Jamal had seen Eyob retreating to Hagos's blue hut, to the bed once owned by Nasnet, the mauve sheets soaked in forbidden love.

Saba couldn't help but wish all wars could end this way, the way Eyob and Hagos had gained their freedom without shedding a drop of blood. Hagos's laughter wafted out of his hut. He giggled. Then he moaned. His words might have been caged forever inside him, his love was not.

Saba retreated inside her hut and from under her bed she pulled out the luggage, full of wedding gifts, and a jute sack containing the second-hand clothes given to her by the aid centre. She sat on her bed, naked between the sack and the luggage, wishing she could wear her own skin until she could buy her own dress. She stayed like this, the breeze stroking her skin, caressing her inner thighs, all day long until the light outside her window faded. The time on her wrist said seven-forty in the evening. Saba headed to the bar, for the drink Azyeb had promised her once she was a married woman. From there, she stuttered to Zahra's hut.

Light beamed through the door Zahra's grandmother always kept open, especially at night. It had become a shelter of safety within the camp. Because, the grandmother said, women flee their husbands mostly by night.

Saba peeked through. She noticed the grandmother and a few girls sitting on a blanket. Zahra stood next to the pole with a tape player in hand. She pressed the play button. Her mother spoke: Zahra, my daughter, first, I want to share a thought. My fight is not only about freeing my country, it is also about freeing me from the chains of my own people. I will not go back to a country I helped free if my people are not free from their prejudice. I'd rather be free in this wilderness than oppressed in my own land which I and my comrades helped liberate.

Zahra turned the tape off just as Saba pushed the door open.

Zahra looked away from the new bride. But her grandmother stood up and welcomed Saba with a song:

My sweetheart whose fate insists
on paving her path with thorns
How do you keep walking?

Saba, unable to hold back her tears, bowed her head. Zahra, come and greet your sister, said the grandmother. I am as upset as you are, but I trust Saba. She agreed to marry for a reason.

Wasn't it you, Grandmother, who told us the time has passed that girls should concede their ambitions for others?

Talk to Saba, not to me, the grandmother said.

Turning to the girls, the grandmother asked them to come with her and leave the two friends alone.

She closed the door behind her. Saba stumbled as she entered the hut and stood next to Zahra.

Did you have a drink?

Saba nodded and leaned against the pole.

You surprise me, Saba, Zahra said, putting the tape player on the ground. I mean, you didn't even resist your mother, you didn't even try to persuade her to change her mind. Zahra paused and took a deep breath. I thought you would protest. What happened to the future you are working to save towards?

Do you think I would get far by washing clothes?

We all have to start somewhere. You said it yourself, Saba. But you gave in to your mother and the midwife.

Saba looked into Zahra's eyes. Zahra, I am not being defeated by my mother, tradition or anyone. I am being practical. I am a refugee living in a refugee camp. Nothing meaningful happens here.

What about school? The aid workers even said that once a school opens here, they will send the best students to the city. And you told me you were always the best in your school back home.

The aid workers have said this since day one. The clinic, the school, the improvement of hygiene, permits to be able to travel: none of these happened. I am trapped here, so what's the difference if I move my unattainable dreams with me to someone else's compound?

God damn this country.

Zahra's shouting drew a crowd. Heads appeared outside the window. The door was flung open by a group of kids. Tell me, Zahra, why is it this country's fault? Saba asked, continuing their private conversation in the presence of strangers.

What land of people would have the heart to put us in this camp?

Ask yourself why we are here, said Saba.

Where does your love for this country come from, Saba? We have never even met its people. Never lived among them.

Saba didn't respond.

I need to be by myself now, said Zahra.

Saba staggered out of Zahra's hut and headed home. Home, she repeated her thought out loud.

Home.

At home, her watch showed it was ten o'clock in the evening. Saba was hanging thinly sliced meat on the clothesline under the full moon, so it would dry overnight, when Zahra stepped into the compound. She was holding a bag.

Saba wept as she threw herself into her friend's arms. Please, don't cry. But Zahra's pleas only provoked more tears.

Saba pulled back from Zahra's embrace and said, I am about to cook something delicious that Hagos taught me. Come eat with me.

I will cook, said Zahra. You are the bride after all.

As Zahra stirred a pot of shoro with meat on the stove, Saba held her hand. And the two friends fell silent. It was this silence that allowed love to foster in this place, root itself in people's hearts as though chests were fertile soil.

The breeze wafted over the compound. The charcoal under the pot glowed. Bubbles popped up in the pot on the fire. The shoro sauce began to splatter. It's ready, said Zahra, let us eat.

Steam rose from the plate as she spread the stew over the injera.

But Saba saw a scorpion climbing up the mud wall of Hagos's hut. One moment, she said to Zahra.

She walked over to the blue hut, took off her slipper and smacked the scorpion as it was about to enter the window. Hagos and Eyob were out. Nasnet's bed was still inhabited though. Saba believed that every act of secret love rumbled long after the act itself was over, like ghosts making their presence felt in the shadows.

She joined Zahra again, pulling her stool closer to the plate. Tearing a piece of injera, she added extra chilli and dipped it in the sauce.

Be careful, you will soon be pregnant, Zahra said.

Saba chuckled. Do you really think I will?

That's what happens after one marries, said Zahra. And in a camp, it is the only thing to happen fast.

Nothing in this compound is what it seems, Saba said. We do our love differently here.

Zahra nodded and Saba felt she had understood.

After tea, Saba and Zahra brought the bed out into the cool compound. They lay on their backs, side by side, facing the illuminated sky, cool air drifting past their touching cheekbones. Both sighed, exhaled. Saba felt Zahra's ribcage expanding against hers.

You are the last person I thought would marry. I know what you are going to say: I did it for Hagos. But the days we girls do things for our families are over. I try to learn selfishness from my mother. Without it, she wouldn't have left me when I was still young to go to fight.

Saba turned her head to look at Zahra. When she stared at her friend, she noticed something for the first time. The miracle of this place was that she could continue to discover new and special things about the same person. Like everything else, observing beauty in people and in what was around you was rationed too.

Saba touched the birthmark on Zahra's left eyelid. Zahra's face had stayed the same since they planted orange seeds on their first day in the camp. Her soldier mother would still recognize her whenever the time came for their reunion. Even in the afterlife.

As if she could read Saba's thoughts, Zahra sighed and said, Anyway, I feel my mother is dead and our country is still occupied and I am in a camp. I don't want my life to be a tragedy after all she has sacrificed.

We will make sure it won't, said Saba.

Zahra lifted her head off the bed and placed it on Saba's chest. I love your heart, she said.

Saba rolled to her side and put an arm around Zahra just as Tedros stormed through the gate with his friends, shouting and laughing. Saba and Zahra sat up. Saba followed Tedros with her eyes as he placed chairs against the wall of his hut. The line of men faced the two young women. As well as the praise poet, there were a few other men Saba had seen at the bar. Tea, said Tedros, clicking his finger at Saba. Move it.

Saba didn't move.

Are you deaf, girl? Tea?

Saba pulled Zahra back. Don't, she said. I will do it.

And when she brought tea to the men, Tedros asked Saba to put the tray with small cups and a pot on the floor. Here, he said, grabbing her wrist.

With his other hand, he took the white cloth out of his shirt pocket and placed it on his crotch. Without looking away from Saba, and with his nails digging into her skin, Tedros ordered the poet to recite a poem about her body.

Saba felt the poet's eyes on her back, his voice rising as they rolled down her hips. The white flag, the sign of her impurity, or his father's impotence, rose towards her when Tedros ordered the poet to stop and for all the men to leave. Now.

He let go of Saba. His eyes moved from his father's wife to Zahra, as he fiddled with the cloth and charged towards his hut.

I am not leaving you alone, Zahra said, when Saba urged her to go. My mother would kill me if I let you face this man on your own.

My husband and brother will be back any moment now from their walk, said Saba. Please, go home. Please.

No, said Zahra. You are not the only stubborn one. I am sleeping in the kitchen.

Before entering the kitchen, Zahra squeezed Saba's hand. Don't worry, everything we face together will be all right.

Saba turned towards Tedros. He stood up and went inside his hut, carrying his jug of beer. He slammed the door shut. And soon after, Saba was awoken by a scream. She jumped out of her bed and ran outside. A red cloth hung between the thinly sliced meat from the clothesline in front of her hut. Blood dripped onto the moonlit ground. The gate was open. High-pitched cries came out of Tedros's hut. Saba rushed inside and found Zahra on the floor. Help me, Saba, she said. Please help me.

FREEDOM: THE DOUBLE PRICE

Saba stood in front of Hajj Ali. They were surrounded by grass, shrubs. This was the field where the aid workers promised to build a school. Saba looked at the rock where she usually sat.

This place is not for love, the nomad said. I know a cave full of jasmine flowers. A woman deserves to lie in a bed of flowers.

Saba's chest heaved. Hajj Ali reached with his hand and massaged her chest, between her breasts, as if to unclog her airways, as he tried to open his own zipper.

Take off your clothes.

There are two conditions, she said, her voice low, barely able to breathe. She turned her head away from him.

He nodded without smiling. Say them then.

A light wind had risen and Saba heard it rustle through the field. First, Saba said, you can't have my vagina. Because I will never let a man I don't love inside me that way.

It was when Saba revealed the second, that Zahra would leave with them so she could be treated in a village for the wounds Tedros had inflicted upon her, that Hajj Ali insisted on a new deal.

Saba hadn't seen the nomad's hunger for Hagos coming. His

desire for her brother was as invisible as Hagos was to the people in the camp.

To smuggle two out of a camp is high risk, Hajj Ali said. I can only do it if I get Hagos as well as you.

Of course not, Saba said to Hajj Ali. It's only me or nothing.

Then I have to go, he said. We will see each other in the camp for the rest of our lives now that you will be staying. My greetings to your husband.

Hajj Ali, wait. Please understand, Zahra needs a doctor urgently or she will die. Please.

It was the morning after Tedros had fled the camp on foot, leaving Zahra behind fighting for her life. Saba and Hagos left their hut for a walk. Clouds obscured the morning sun. They climbed the hill, the same hill on which they had sat on that first morning in the camp. Flowers tickled Saba's feet. Hot wind blew. Saba studied the profile of Hagos's face as he stared out to the camp. His hair fluttered against his face.

A moth landed on her shoulder and spread its wings. Insects climbed her feet. She had become a habitat for wilderness just as the wilderness was her habitat.

Saba took the map from under her bra and showed it to Hagos.

Six hours. Yes, it would take me six hours to get to the village by cart, Saba said to Hagos. She whispered to him her new dream, because the old Saba she had dreamed was no longer feasible. Saba is leaving the camp to fight. She had made the promise to Zahra that if anything was to happen to her, she would take her place.

But he set a heavy price, she said to Hagos. A price we both have to pay to Hajj Ali. And I will never let you do this.

Hagos pulled her closer to him. They wrapped their arms around each other and their cheeks pressed together, like the intertwined flowers her grandmother had planted on the wall of their courtyard back home.

LOVE SHARED

Hagos was asleep alongside Eyob. Both men shared the habit of heavy sleeping, as if, Saba thought, they were in one long, deep dream which ought not be interrupted. As if their love could only come alive in the hours when the midwife, the judge, the mother, the committee of elders were asleep, in the hours when tradition closed its eyes, leaving desire free and unhindered.

Saba lay next to Eyob. She emulated her brother and placed an arm on her husband's chest. This was her time to be loved.

We all entered this camp as humans but only some of us would leave so. Disgust is an acquired taste, she reminded herself.

But this wasn't disgusting. It astonished Saba how judgemental thoughts still arrived in her mind and how much resisting she still had to do. Eyob was the oasis in which both she and her brother took refuge from their long journey. His heart, the heart that had stopped twice before, beat under his ribcage, rhythmically.

Saba undressed and squeezed herself between the two men.

THE DEPARTURE

At the crack of dawn Saba arrived at Hajj Ali's compound as the nomad descended from his barn at the top of the hill, where she saw the long slender shadow of her brother rising to his feet. The animals around Hagos scurried, ramming heads and horns against each other and the cage.

Hagos had gone to see Hajj Ali before dawn, when, said the nomad, darkness would shield them from view. But Saba remembered the imam's words to her on the first day in the camp: God is everywhere. The first flicker of light appeared in the sky. As if, Saba thought, he lit the wick of the universe, longing to be seen now, now that it was over.

And it was at that time of the morning when the camp was just beginning to emerge from darkness, when the streak of a flame split the sky, that Hajj Ali parted the legs of his goat. Let me finish milking and we will leave, he said to Saba.

Saba looked at the picture of the graduate and folded the newspaper which the Khwaja had insisted she take with her as a reminder of her dream, now shelved. For ever, perhaps. When the goat kicked, Hajj Ali placed one of her legs over his shoulder and wrapped his fingers around her teat. Milk splattered into his bowl.

Saba studied his appearance. The face that she once thought reflected nature, as if refined by the constant wind against which he travelled, seemed fuller and lighter. For someone who was supposed to be a traveller, he had become rooted in the camp. He had established a monopoly over the production of meat and dairy. His roosters roamed the field, next to the large chicken cage, inside which Saba could see many eggs. His daughter sold milk by going hut to hut, his wife churned the remainder into butter for making ga'at porridge as well as oiling the hair, and he had set up a makeshift slaughterhouse, selling meat in affordable portions.

Saba's sun-strained eyes looked over to her left at the animal skins treated with salt. They had multiple uses: they were used as mattresses and seating rugs, as well as praying mats. Saba remembered it was she and the businessman who had persuaded Hajj Ali to stay. But then she noticed the donkey at the bottom of a hill, the donkey that would lead her and Zahra out of the camp.

The goat hobbled. But Hajj Ali was as steady as the rock on which he sat. When he finished milking, the goat trudged away, then rushed to her flock in the barn, where Hagos was rubbing mud off his chest.

Of course, she cried.

i do it will, I wrote to Saba in the broken English she taught me, a language that was foreign and new to us both and that we spoke as though we had regressed to the time we ought to have spoken it first as toddlers.

no, she wrote back, never let i you this do

but saba say you not always we same are that our bodies same are feel you pain when feel i pain we one are one we are

When she hugged me after reading my note, whispering in my ears, oh Hagosey, I love you, I tell you, I felt as broken as the words we spoke, as unnatural as the foreign language we tried to root in us. A day would come, though, we both said to one another, when we would tell our history, recount this time in our own language. But that day would be when we returned to our country, the country Saba was on her way to fight for in Zahra's place.

As Hajj Ali rose from me, I stayed supine on the ground of the barn, remembering Tahir, the lorry driver, and the words he said to Saba as he asked her to keep the seeds from the orange he gave to us, so she would plant it in the camp: Our country, Saba, is like any in the world, there are good and bad people. I hope and pray you won't have to pay a high price to leave the camp.

I wished he'd made that same prayer for me too.

Dung. Dung everywhere. Around me. And on me. The smell of that first time we entered the camp wafted to me from my chest that Hajj Ali had squeezed with his hands smeared in manure, from the barn where I lay, from my face, my feet. It was as if I was a hut, a camp built with animal remains to last in this wilderness.

Dawn embraced me now. I stood still in the barn looking at my sister next to the nomad. He drank some of the milk from his goat and passed the bowl to Saba as he munched on some dates, thanking God, his voice reaching my ears, as if I was Saba near him. He thanked Mother Nature. And in the camp, nature possessed tenderness. I wept as Saba wrapped her arms around herself. In the same way I did.

The donkey brayed. Come, let's go, Hajj Ali called to my sister as he pulled the cart and linked it to the reins around the donkey. He wound his turban and, looking at the sky, he spread his hands in prayer: May God make our path ahead safe.

Saba stroked the donkey's face and wiped the secretion from its eyes, for the road ahead, for the journey ahead, for the life ahead. Fighters don't cry, I wanted to shout. But then she was a human being first. She freed herself before her country, she freed me, and freed love in our compound, in our camp, before she set off on her way to the front to pick up a gun to free a piece of land.

Saba jumped on the cart next to Hajj Ali, her legs dangling over the large wheels. The nomad smacked the donkey's back with his long stick and the cart edged forward. I followed it as it turned right, plodded up a hill and then slowly trekked over the narrow passage, and into lanes onto which wafted heavy breathings, moans, baby cries, dreams spoken loud, stories told to the ghosts, and when it entered the square, the cart sped up past the imam, who was about to enter the mosque with his oil lamp. Then it stopped.

Holding the hands of her grandmother and the Khwaja, Zahra limped past the aid centre, as if she were carrying Tedros on her back.

Let's go. Hajj Ali's voice rose as he pulled the reins, swinging his whip so it sliced the air. The donkey moved forward, then bolted off through the square. A flicker of light trickled through my mother's hut.

As the donkey cart drove past the aid centre, Eyob ran into the square and came to stand next to me. He waved with the note Saba had left him. I moved my lips. I love you too, Saba said, taking a final look at me, as I became visible in the glow of the man I loved, as I loved her.

The graduate girl on the British newspaper quivered on Saba's lap. Saba loosened her grip. Dreams for a woman are no longer inherited but created, she'd said. The paper flew out of her hand. It sailed onto the ground and rested on a thorny shrub. I picked it up.

Saba placed an arm around Zahra and her friend rested her head on my sister's chest. Saba turned her face towards their destination, the path that would take her back to her country, still at war, across this vast, open land of Sudan, full of generous people.

ACKNOWLEDGEMENTS

To my mother – Sadiyah: I thank you for taking me out of the refugee camp and saving my life. But the timing couldn't have been more wrong. It happened just as I was falling in love for the first time!

To my grandmother – Mebrat: thank you for bringing me up, for teaching me how to make zigni stew and for allowing me to be quiet when I didn't want to talk as a child. You saw that silence was my mother tongue.

My friends know now why I also call myself Sulaiman Sadiyah-Mebrat.

Lies Craeynest, I'm so grateful for all your support, for standing by me, and for reading time and again. Amira and Saleh Addonia, sorry I moved away from London, from you, but thank you for always supporting me, you are my inspiration. Minna Salami, whose meditation tips helped when editing this novel: thank you for being there for me.

My son, who raged at me last year that this book was as old as him and still not finished. I didn't put you in time-out then, because you being an Arsenal fan is punishing enough.

My daughter, who teaches me 'how' to dance all the time. 'It's like this, Daddy, not like that.'

Massive appreciation to Ellah Wakatama Allfrey. It's been a dream working with you.

Isobel Dixon, thank you for believing in this book. Lisa Classen, Susanna Nicklin, Maaza Mengiste, Michael Salu, Vimbai Shire, Alexander Spears, Lee Gillette, Ubah Cristina Ali Farah, Kate Vrielynck, Geert Craeynest, Tamara Gaussi, Anne Bathily, big thank you all. I wrote this book, mainly, around cafes in Ixelles, Brussels, so thanks to all baristas who became friends.

Hawa Addonia, rest in peace my beautiful sister. I love you.

Karen Goeyens, may you rest in peace our dear friend.

To young Sulaiman: those multiple childhood traumas resurfaced aggressively during the writing of this book, reminding me how much you've endured. Thank you.

ABOUT THE AUTHOR

Sulaiman S.M.Y. Addonia is a novelist who fled Eritrea as a refugee in childhood. He spent his early life in a refugee camp in Sudan following the Om Hajar massacre in 1976, and in his early teens he lived and studied in Jeddah, Saudi Arabia. He arrived in London as an unaccompanied minor without a word of English and went on to earn a BSc in Economics from University College London and an MA in Development Studies from the School of Oriental and African Studies, University of London. His debut novel, *The Consequences of Love*, was shortlisted for the Commonwealth Writers' Prize and was translated into more than twenty languages. He currently lives in Brussels where he has launched a creative writing academy for refugees and asylum seekers.

The text of *Silence Is My Mother Tongue*
is set in Goudy Old Style.
Book design by www.salu.io.
Composition by Beyond White Space.
Manufactured by Versa Press on acid-free,
30 percent postconsumer wastepaper.